His hands went over her roughly, urgently . . .

As he pulled her into his arms, she unashamedly burrowed even closer, reveling in his male strength. All she wanted was to stay in that passionate embrace, pulsingly aware of the heat of his body as she clung to him. And then he bent to kiss her, possessively, lingeringly, blotting out all memory of the past, all thought of the future. . . .

MASTER
OF
LOVE

∞

by

Glenna Finley

A SIGNET BOOK

NEW AMERICAN LIBRARY

TIMES MIRROR

NAL BOOKS ARE ALSO AVAILABLE AT DISCOUNTS IN BULK
QUANTITY FOR NDUSTRIAL OR SALES-PROMOTIONAL USE.
FOR DETAILS, WRITE TO PREMIUM MARKETING DIVISION,
NEW AMERICAN LIBRARY, INC., 1301 AVENUE OF THE
AMERICAS, NEW YORK, NEW YORK 10019.

SIGNET TRADEMARK REG. U.S. PAT. OFF. AND FOREIGN COUNTRIES
REGISTERED TRADEMARK—MARCA REGISTRADA
HECHO EN CHICAGO, U.S.A.

SIGNET, SIGNET CLASSICS, MENTOR, PLUME AND
MERIDIAN BOOKS are published by
The New American Library, Inc.,
1301 Avenue of the Americas, New York, New York 10019

FIRST SIGNET PRINTING, APRIL, 1978

1 2 3 4 5 6 7 8 9

PRINTED IN THE UNITED STATES OF AMERICA

Chapter One

"How do you open the knot?"

The unexpected question made Jennifer Rogers turn from the colorful scene in front of her to the slight figure of a teen-aged girl by her side. "I beg your pardon?" she asked.

"How do you open the knot?" the girl repeated in a heavily accented tone. She indicated the rope barrier separating them from the top of the steep basket-sled ride for which the Portuguese island of Madeira was famous.

A tall man who was at Jennifer's other side cut in smoothly. "You don't open the knot here," he advised the confused girl. "You go around past the restaurant door over there and see the man wearing a cap. He'll put you in the basket."

A relieved smile lightened the girl's face. "*Efkharisto*," she began and then changed to, "Thank you. You have been kind. Good-bye."

The man nodded casually and watched her move away before directing his attention to Jennifer. "I didn't mean to interfere," he explained, "but you looked a little puzzled."

She was still staring dazedly at the rope.

1

"Open the knot," she murmured. "What kind of dialect is that? I've never heard the expression."

"Neither have I, but she's probably only had three months of English. Besides, if you think about it—why not open a knot? That's all you do when you untie it."

"It sounds reasonable," she confessed after thinking it over. Then she made a wry grimace. "I'm not usually so slow on the uptake, but I just arrived here a while ago and my mind's still in a jet fog." She started to turn away when his next words stopped her.

"I was watching you in the restaurant. Frankly, I'm surprised you're indulging in a wine-tasting party halfway up a mountainside on your first day in Madeira. I should think you'd be resting at your hotel."

"I don't intend to take to my bed just because I lost a little sleep." She tried to keep her tone pleasantly unconcerned. "And it was only a thimbleful of madeira wine that the guide gave us. You don't have to make it sound like an orgy."

He considered her speculatively. "My good girl, I wasn't delivering a temperance lecture. When we were in there watching that native dancing, I noticed you looked a little pale. It's just as well you came out to get some fresh air." He gave her a brief nod and moved over to take a picture of the garden beyond the path.

Jennifer's gray-green eyes flashed with annoyance. At twenty-three, and possessed with a figure and profile beyond reproach, she was unaccustomed to masculine criticism of any kind. Inwardly she knew that the stranger was probably right; she'd seen smudges under her eyes but she hadn't wanted to miss any of the excitement during her short stay on the fabled vacation island. Instead, she'd taken a cold shower in her hotel room and decided to ignore her weariness. Jet lag was only partially responsible for her condition—the rest was reaction from her brother Jeremy's bout with peritonitis in Paris. Surgery in the American Hospital there had brought that emergency to a happy conclusion, and when she had left France the day before, Jeremy had been recovering nicely.

"I'm sorry about foisting this detour to Madeira on you," he told Jennifer on her last visit, "but I'd hate to blow my chances completely with Dr. Whitney. It was pure luck getting appointed with him in the first place—just the data I needed for my thesis."

"Don't worry about it. There are lots of other scientists working on foundation grants in the Mediterranean besides Reed Whitney—you said so yourself. There'll be other chances for you later on."

He'd merely frowned at her platitudes. "Not with a man like him. He doesn't bother with an assistant most of the time. Don't you remember, he did that last work in Zaire all alone." As she looked puzzled, he continued, "When he was checking to see what effect hydroelectric construction on the Nile would have on the ecology of the region."

She looked at him in amusement. "I've never heard of it. It'll never make the best-seller list."

"That's because most people don't know how important it is," he insisted staunchly. "I tell you, Whitney's absolute tops in his field."

Jennifer hastened to calm Jeremy before he worked himself into a relapse while defending his academic idol. "No doubt he's terrific—I'm just the wrong type to appreciate men with scientific minds. Other than yours," she added, smiling down at him. "And you're in the family so there's no escape." Then she frowned slightly, "I thought you and Whitney were going to work near the mouth of the Nile on this trip."

"We were." A disgruntled expression settled over his features. "The Egyptians have already drawn most of their conclusions there—Whitney and I were going to meet with government officials and check the latest statistics. Our foundation has been retained to see if the benefits of the Aswan Dam will outweigh the ecological damage that it's caused."

"You may be strong enough to hold a discussion on ecology this morning, but I'm not," Jennifer told him firmly. "I walked through three acres in the Louvre yesterday after I visited you."

"For pete's sake, you didn't have to do everything in one day," he told her with brotherly candor. "Paris will still be here when you get back from Madeira."

"Secretaries don't get foundation grants—just three-week vacations."

"I'll trade your salary for mine, anytime," he said. "Besides, that boss of yours would give you two months off at full salary if he thought he'd make you happy. Why don't you marry him and put him out of his misery?"

"Because I don't love him. You know all about that and so does he. Stop trying to change the subject, if you want me to catch my plane. Just tell me again what I'm supposed to do in Madeira."

"Find Dr. Whitney at Reid's Hotel and give him my apologies."

"All right, but I still don't see why you're worried. No one could blame you for getting appendicitis."

He had the grace to flush. "It isn't that simple. The darned appendix had been grumbling for the past month, but when this chance to work with Whitney came up, I tried to bluff it through."

"Honestly, Jeremy—you're an idiot. What if you'd had this attack when you were wandering around the wilds of Egypt!"

"Well, I didn't—so stop fussing. For lord's sake, Jenny, you're only ten minutes older than I am—not ten years. Just take the plane to Madeira and give the man my apologies. If you can charm him the way you do all the men in that advertising agency of yours, it'll be better still. That way, maybe I can get a chance to work with him next spring if he's in the Mediterranean again."

"What's Dr. Whitney doing on Madeira if he's going to work in Egypt?" Jennifer asked, leaning over to smooth the white counterpane of her brother's hospital bed.

"I don't know. Vacationing, I suppose. Maybe he has a blonde stashed there that he visits between field trips."

She was quick to catch the note of weariness that was creeping into his voice, and she cast an anxious glance at him even as she said, "It doesn't matter. The egghead can have a whole quiverful of Portuguese beauties to cheer his off-hours if he wants." She smiled down at Jeremy. "It's just a good thing for you that I've always wanted to spend a day or so in Madeira. I wouldn't have helped you if Doctor Whitney had been keeping company with mosquitoes in central Africa."

"Yes, you would," her twin said flatly. "You always have. Sometime I'll buy you a cup of coffee to make up for it."

"Then wait till we get home. If I have one more cup of French coffee, I'll be too weak to make my plane."

With that, she'd left him smiling, but she was still worried enough about his condition that she'd called Paris as soon as she checked in at her hotel in Funchal the next day. It wasn't until she heard that Jeremy was continuing to recover without complications that she was able to take in the magnificence of her surroundings for the first time.

When her flight landed on Madeira at dawn, Jennifer had been too sleepy to appreciate the rich green vegetation covering the mountain ridges still partially shrouded by an early morning mist. The ride in from the airport had given only a brief glimpse of the brilliant flowers decorating the countryside. As they reached Funchal, Jennifer's eyes had widened at the bright purple and red bougainvillea canopies covering each garden wall and the earthenware containers full of scarlet geraniums and yellow cannas around even the most modest hillside huts.

When she saw the floral plantings surrounding the resort hotels, she began to understand why the island had remained so popular with voyagers ever since its discovery in 1419.

It was the thought of exploring the "Pearl of the Atlantic," where Christopher Columbus married and lived before his American voyages, that made Jennifer linger just long enough in her hotel room to get cleaned up and admire her view over an emerald swimming pool before starting out to discover what the island offered.

The man on the hotel's reception desk assured her that the most popular feature of the island was the basket-sledge ride down the mountainside. "Absolutely not to be missed," he emphasized.

"It sounds wonderful. I'd love to try it!" Jennifer said, her weariness forgotten. She had a momentary twinge of conscience when she thought of Jeremy's instructions and then decided Reed Whitney would probably still be asleep at that early hour. A middle-aged scientist recovering from an arduous African field trip would need all the rest he could get. He certainly wouldn't appreciate being awakened just to hear that his assistant wasn't going to arrive.

A last-minute surge of caution made her linger by the reception desk. It wouldn't hurt to be sure of her facts. "Do you have a Dr. Whitney staying here?" she asked. "A Dr. Reed Whitney."

The clerk thumbed through some registration cards and nodded. "Dr. Whitney checked into the hotel three days ago."

"Good . . ."

"But I don't think he's available just now," he continued with a glance at his watch. "Perhaps later."

"Just as I thought." Jennifer smiled and slid her sunglasses onto her nose. "I'll get in touch with him this afternoon."

"Would you like to leave a note?"

"No, thanks." Jeremy's instructions made her voice firm. "I'd prefer to see him personally."

"It wouldn't be difficult now if you'd like to wait . . ."

"After the basket-sledge ride will be plenty of time. Is there anything else that's fun to do while I'm on the island?"

The young man behind the desk became expansive. "There's a night club up in the village of Canico. The music is distinctive and the dancers are very popular with our visitors. "

Jennifer shook her head. "I'm traveling alone—I don't think a night club would be a good idea."

"Allow me to arrange it for you." He leaned over the counter. "I promise you'll remember it all your life."

She was too tired to argue. "All right. Just leave a map in my mailbox showing how to get there. I'll pick it up when I come back this afternoon." She settled a floppy-brimmed straw hat on her head. "Can I hire a car to take me up to the basket place?"

He beamed with satisfaction. "There are taxis just outside the door. You will enjoy the day, Miss Rogers. I am sure of it."

Jennifer would have been the first to agree with him as she was driven through Funchal's busy streets and then on up a winding road through the city's suburbs, where small villas clung to the edge of the hillside. The taxi passed tiny cars that sounded as if they were powered by rubber-band motors and occasional buses that struggled to negotiate the steep

grade and sharp curves. At the roadside, hibis-
cus and oleander shrubbery eventually gave
way to mimosa and eucalyptus when they
reached higher altitudes. Jennifer saw the tree
branches bend under the stiff breeze that had
appeared from nowhere and wished belatedly
that she'd brought along a sweater.

Fortunately, they arrived at the three-thou-
sand-foot summit where the basket-sledge ride
started before she had time to dwell on her
mistake.

The taxidriver let her off at the back of a
large stone building which he assured her was
a fine restaurant.

"I don't want to eat," she protested. "I just
want to go down in a basket."

The man's English was limited, but he
caught the gist of her words. He pointed
toward the watch on his wrist and indicated
thirty minutes. "Not now. You wait in building."

Jennifer sighed and capitulated. The sun had
disappeared behind a cloud and it was far too
chilly to stand around in the wind which was
now manipulating the tree branches like stick
figures. She had to clutch her hat to keep her
shoulder-length brown hair in any semblance
of order.

When she'd stepped hesitantly into the big
whitewashed room at the front of the restaurant, she'd been welcomed by the proprietor,

who thrust a glass of madeira wine into her hand.

"It's too early for wine," she protested as the man moved her to an empty table near the dance floor. "I haven't even had breakfast."

"Who needs food?" he said practically. "Enjoy the wine. We have special prices for visitors. You can decide what kind to buy while you watch the dancers."

"But I just want to take the basket-sledge ride." Jennifer lowered her voice as she noticed amused glances from the rest of the patrons at tables nearby. Clearly they weren't objecting to the wine-tasting party.

"Later, madam," the proprietor told her firmly. "You can't hurry these things."

Even a few sips of madeira couldn't put any gloss on the dance program that followed. The recital was staged by eight costumed teenagers who obviously weren't entranced by shuffling in circles at that time of the morning for tourists who should know better. The dancers' expressions showed it; so did their measured stomps to the rhythm of a *brinquinho*—a kind of tambourine music-maker. For the first time since she'd arrived, Jennifer began to wish that she'd been less impulsive and taken time for breakfast in the hotel before her mad dash up the mountain.

When the folk dancers went into a third apathetic chorus, she yawned and took another sip of the madeira wine before letting her gaze move around the room.

It stopped abruptly on a dark-haired man standing at the bar whose six-foot height made him loom over the stocky Portuguese bartender who was talking to him. The stranger was deeply tanned and wearing sunglasses that masked his expression, but there was a studied assurance in his manner that put him in his early thirties at least. His cotton shirt and slacks didn't help identify his nationality, nor did the small canvas rucksack he was carrying. Jennifer abruptly moved her attention back to the dancers when the man's mocking expression showed that he was aware of her interest. She kept her glance on the dance floor after that until the dancers finally finished and bowed to polite applause.

When she stood up and started for the restaurant door, she managed a careless look over her shoulder and found the stranger starting to follow. She only had time to note the European cut of his yellow sports shirt before she escaped through a convenient side door. He was too tall for a Frenchman or Italian, she decided, and wearing the wrong clothes for an Englishman. That only left a Scandinavian or a rangy Australian. She smiled slightly as she made her way down the path toward the beginning of the basket ride. Too bad that she'd never know. Someone should have told the stranger that it was the wrong time and place for a casual pickup. An American man would have known that he'd have better luck at a coffee bar.

Even the fleeting thought of a steaming cup of coffee made Jennifer hasten her steps. There might be a chance to find one at the bottom of the ride, she decided, when a quick glance at her watch showed that the basket men must be open for business at last.

At the end of the path, a knotted rope barred her way from the steep cobblestone path that started down the mountainside. There was a flurry of activity to her left where the straw-hatted porters dressed in white shirts and pants were readying the wicker basket chairs mounted on greased runners. There were short ropes on either side so that the men could guide the sled down the course and enough room on the back of the wooden runners so that they could ride on the steeper sections, in the manner of Alaskan sled-dog drivers. Jennifer was caught up in the excitement of it when the woman at her side had said. "How do you open the knot?" and started the whole thing.

"You'd better go back and sit down for a while in that restaurant." The tall stranger who had followed her and solved the knot query was back beside her. He took her elbow as he said reprovingly, "You must be half asleep by now."

She shook off his grasp. "I'm perfectly fine."

"You mean that you go into a fog every time somebody strikes up a conversation?"

Jennifer looked up at him coolly, noting the network of fine lines on his skin at the edge of his sunglasses. She'd been right about his age; the rucksack might carry a pair of tennis shoes, but he wasn't a student on a university holiday. He wasn't foreign either; the approach was all too familiar. She said quite definitely, "I thought you'd get the drift by now that I'm not interested. It's nothing personal," she went on, softening her tone, "but there's no point in wasting your time. I'm just going to be on the island for a day or two because I have to meet a man."

His dark eyebrows went up. "I see."

"No, you don't. It isn't that kind of a thing. This is strictly business—not that it's any of yours," she added, noting his amusement. "Anyhow, all I want to do right now is take one of these baskets down the mountain and find a cup of coffee afterward."

He nodded slowly. "Well, would you mind if I shared your ride?" He indicated the beginning of the course. "They prefer to have two people in a basket."

"I don't mind at all." She tilted her head back to look up at him. "Just so long as you know the score—there's no future in it."

"You've gotten that point across loud and clear," he acknowledged as they waited behind a half-dozen stragglers from a German tour group. "Better get your ticket ready," he said as they neared the head of the line.

"Ticket?" Her fingers went up to her mouth in consternation. "Is that what the sign says? I didn't know you needed one."

"Don't worry—it's only twenty *escudos* . . ."

"*Escudos?*" she parroted again. "Oh, help! I forgot to change my money. The taxidriver took American bills. Maybe they'll let me . . ."

"Not here," he told her firmly. "You'd have to go back in the restaurant. Unless you'll permit me . . ." He dug into his pocket and pulled out a handful of Portuguese coins.

"Would you?" she entreated. "I'd be very grateful."

"Certainly." His tone was solemn. "But only if you understand that I'm not setting a precedent. There's absolutely no future in it."

Despite the confusion around them, she shook her head slowly. "Oh, lord, did I sound *that* stuffy? I'd better apologize."

"Another time." He grinned and pushed her toward a basket that two porters had readied at the top of the course. "Watch your step now—these cobbles are slick as the devil. Even if you only have two days here"—he paid the ticketseller and helped her into the padded basket seat—"you certainly don't have time for a broken leg. Now, hang on!" He arranged his own long legs so that she was braced firmly in place as their two runners grasped the ropes on either side and took up their positions.

"You sound as if you'd done this before," Jennifer managed to get out even as the runners gave a mighty shove and the sled gathered speed on the steep, narrow path down the mountainside. "Oh," she caught her breath sharply as the basket careened even faster and fishtailed into the first curve.

"Allow me." There was a definite undercurrent of amusement in his voice as he put a strong arm around her shoulders and pulled her tightly against him. "Now there's no chance of your flying out into that ditch." He jerked a thumb toward the stream of water cascading down the mountainside at the left of the path, while he tactfully ignored the sheer drop on the right. Then the scenery whizzed by in a merciful blur as the runners urged even greater speed. A moment later there was the smell of smoke when the wooden glides under the sled started smoldering until the gradient lessened and the men holding the ropes were able to run alongside on the cobbles again.

The man sitting beside Jennifer must have heard her relieved sigh because he relaxed his grip on her shoulder and said conversationally, "The people who lived up here must have had a quick trip to work in the old days. I wonder how much longer it took them to get home?"

Jennifer tore her gaze from the winding path still ahead of them. "I don't understand. You mean this wasn't set up for the tourists?"

"Not at all. Apparently all the people who had homes up here arranged to have sled runners take them to work in the morning."

She tried not to notice that their speed was increasing again as they got through a curve and started down the straightaway. "Well, it's a lot faster than a Fifth Avenue bus."

"And probably safer," he said as they passed a wide spot on the path where three women were kneeling to wash clothes in the rushing waters of the stream.

Jennifer glanced back in amazement until the path turned again and the women were out of sight. "I didn't think I'd see that here."

"Madeira hasn't changed much since the old days. There's still an Edwardian atmosphere around here—more than in Portugal itself. It wasn't too long ago that you could still be carried up this mountainside in a hammock."

"You have to be kidding!"

His palm went up. "Word of honor. It was the height of luxury. There were two men—one at each end of the hammock. All you had to do was lie back and relax."

"If I went down the mountain in this basket every day, it wouldn't be long before they carried me out in a hammock," she said, burrowing against him as the sled whistled past wild cane borders when they approached the lower reaches. "I may even need one now to get back to the hotel." She gave a gasp as the sled swerved over a bump and the perspiring runners had to shove it back on the track. Then they clambered on the back again with hardly a missed step. Jennifer bit her lip and tried to laugh. "A roller coaster would seem tame after this. Wait till I find that hotel clerk."

"We're almost at the end. This is Monte." The man beside her removed his arm from her shoulders as the path widened into a cobbled street when they reached the outskirts of the village. As the runners pulled the sled to a gradual stop, he went on, "There are usually taxis waiting in that park in front of the church. I'm going back to Funchal myself if you'd like to share one. Here—hang on to me." The last order came as she stood up, swaying slightly when she tried to step out of the sled.

"I can't think what's the matter with me."

"Just a case where your spirit's willing but your muscles are lagging behind." He kept a hand under her elbow as he turned back to the runners and tipped them.

Their faces split with wide smiles. *"Obrigado, senhor. Boa sorte!"*

"If that means 'come again,' they're out of luck. I wouldn't have missed it, but once was enough, thanks," Jennifer said, moving over to the edge of the cobblestones so that some schoolchildren—neatly dressed in red-, white-, and blue-checked smocks and carrying wicker lunchbaskets—could pass by. "They make a wonderful sight, don't they? All braids and bright, shining faces—just like that old song." She hummed a verse of it as she strolled along beside him through the park in front of a stucco and timbered church. Then she pulled to a stop on the path. "I really should introduce myself ..."

"You don't have to," he cut in quickly. "I haven't forgotten the ground rules. Sharing a taxi into Funchal doesn't change things."

"Whatever you say." She looked amused but obediently walked on until they reached a small bird pond which bordered the path on the other side. "Just a second—I'd like a picture of that little thatch house the ducks use for shelter. Oh, damn!"

He was watching her almost warily. "Now what?"

Jennifer's attention was still on her camera. "I'm at the end of the film. Probably I took too many pictures on the way to the top. Well, it doesn't matter. I can buy a postcard," she said, aware that he had taken his camera out of the case and was, even then, focusing on the scene she'd mentioned. She waited politely until he'd finished.

"I'll send you a print if it's any good," he said almost brusquely as he fell into step beside her.

Jennifer glanced sideways at him, wondering what had caused his abrupt change of attitude. On the sled ride he'd gone out of his way to be considerate and charming. Now he was acting like he couldn't wait to get rid of her. She decided to ignore the warning and smiled up at him. "If you're mailing me a picture, you'll have to know my name and address. I'm Jen-

nifer Rogers from New York—I'll just be at
Reid's Hotel for a day or two until I get in
touch with the man that my brother's supposed
to work for. Incidentally, since you tipped
those basket men, I'll pay for our taxi back to
Funchal."

The man beside her pulled up abruptly in
the middle of the path. From the frown on his
face, it was obvious he wasn't admiring the red
azaleas in full bloom on the hillside nearby.
"What do you mean—supposed to work for?" he
asked tersely.

Jennifer's lips parted and she stared blankly
at him. If he'd suddenly demanded her purse
and her traveler's checks, she couldn't have
been more astounded. "I beg your pardon?"

"I asked what you meant—about your brother
being *supposed to* work for me."

"Not for *you*," she began, "he was going to
work for a Dr. Whit——" Her voice trailed off as
sudden comprehension swept over her. There
was an instant of silence, unbroken except for
the buzzing of a bluebottle fly in the shrubbery
behind them. Then she managed to finish her
sentence, sounding as if she'd swallowed the fly
in the interim. "——for a Dr. Reed Whitney. I
probably should have realized except that I
thought you were still asleep . . . at the hotel. The desk clerk said so . . . almost." She
floundered as his dark eyebrows went up.

"I was down at the pool. Afterward, he told
me there was a young woman named Rogers

who was asking for me. That's why I followed you to the top of the mountain. Where's Jeremy?"

His bald question didn't allow for evasion. "He isn't here," she replied with the same economy of words, "and he's not coming. I'm supposed to tell you."

Reed Whitney stood still, staring down at her. Then his cold glance flickered toward her left hand. "What's your connection with Jeremy—or is that being indelicate?"

"Hardly. He's my brother . . . my twin."

Reed took off his sunglasses and considered her. "You're not much alike," he said finally.

She tried not to laugh. "I really didn't have anything to do with that."

The underlying amusement in her voice didn't improve his temper. "I didn't mean to imply that you had, Miss Rogers. This isn't a laughing matter, however. When you see your brother again, tell him he might give his superior the courtesy of a personal reply the next time he can't fulfill a contract. However, he needn't bother applying to the Foundation in the future." He nodded politely. "Good-bye, Miss Rogers, I'll see that you get a print of that picture you wanted." He turned and started striding down the path toward the taxi rank at the bottom of the hill.

Jennifer stared after him for a horror-stricken moment and then ran to catch up with him. "Dr. Whitney . . . please . . . wait a minute . . . oh!" A sharply protruding rock on the path caught the edge of her heel and made her stumble.

The man in front of her had turned with a frown, which changed to concern as he saw her ankle give way. Quickly he reached back to shore her up. "Are you okay—no, don't try to walk for a minute."

Jennifer shook her head in protest and put her foot down gingerly. "It's not bad . . . it just sort of twinges. In an hour or so, it will be fine. Dr. Whitney, I need to talk to you—you have the wrong idea about Jeremy."

"That's no excuse for making a mad dash on these cobblestones. You're lucky that you didn't break your neck." He kept his arm under hers and maneuvered her around on the path like a recalcitrant child. "Lean on me and try not to use that ankle more than you have to. Where in the devil is that brother of yours?"

"In a Paris hospital." She felt his body stiffen in surprise. "That's what I meant to tell you all along."

"Then you certainly went about it the hard way."

"I know." She rubbed her head wearily. "Sorry, I'm not usually so thick. Jeremy had his appendix removed, but there were complications with peritonitis. He's coming along fine now, though. I checked with the hospital this morning."

"I'm glad to hear it." There was no doubting

the sincerity in Reed Whitney's deep voice. "Then the next thing to do is get you back to the hotel before there are two patients in the Rogers family." He beckoned authoritatively to the first taxi they came to and opened the door when it pulled alongside. "In you go." Before she knew what was happening, he had deposited her effortlessly on the back seat.

Jennifer waited until he'd gotten in on the other side and given the driver the name of the hotel before she said, "How tall are you, for heaven's sake?"

"About six-three, I guess. Why?" He surveyed her with that dispassionate look she'd noticed from the first.

"Jeremy didn't mention that you were so big—or so young." She had trouble staying upright on the vinyl seat as the cabdriver started down a winding road that resembled the basket route.

"I'm sorry that I didn't grow a gray beard for the occasion."

"Well, you certainly could have told me who you were when we met up at that restaurant. I thought you were just trying to pick me up."

"I didn't come near you," he protested mildly.

"You know what I mean."

He shifted slightly on the seat, but she couldn't tell whether he was uncomfortable under her accusation or simply trying to keep his balance as the driver leaned on the horn and shot around a public bus at an intersection. "I was just trying to figure you out," Reed admitted finally. "You'd been so damned elusive at the hotel, I didn't know what you had in mind. From the way you were flitting around, I thought Jeremy had brought a girl friend on the job. Up at the restaurant, I was working on a diplomatic way to get rid of you."

His pronouncement made Jennifer color furiously. "You don't need any elaborate plans for that, Dr. Whitney. I'm just going to be on the island overnight—Jeremy insisted that I come and deliver his apologies in person."

"Very nice of him." He ignored her anger by rolling down the window when the cab stopped for a traffic light, focusing his camera on a wrought-iron gate almost entirely covered by purple and red bougainvillea. Then he sat back and closed the window again as the car started up. "We can discuss it later. Were you vacationing in Europe, Miss Rogers?"

When he addressed her in that pedantic tone, he sounded as if he *should* have a gray beard, Jennifer thought rebelliously. The man couldn't have been more than in his early thirties; there was no reason for him to sound like something out of Dickens. She gave a mental shrug and decided to adopt the same formality. "That's right. I only have three weeks, but I'd arranged to spend some time with Jeremy in Paris before he met you. I hope that you'll be able to make other arrangements for your Egyptian trip, Dr. Whitney."

"Ummm. I'll work on it." He put his camera in its case and reached for his wallet as the cab drew into the circular drive of the hotel. "Take it easy with your ankle—I'll help you in a minute."

"There's no need—it's practically as good as new," Jennifer said, fumbling for the door handle and stepping carefully down onto the drive.

Reed gave her an admonishing look from the other side of the taxi, but he didn't say anything more until he'd paid the driver and the car had driven off. Then he walked around to where she was waiting by the door of the hotel and guided her into the lobby. "Don't you ever do anything that you're told?"

It was an offhand comment, but it made Jennifer pull up in the big, high-ceilinged foyer, ignoring the bustle of hotel guests around them. "Only when someone employs me," she told him coolly and extended her hand. "It's been nice meeting you, Dr. Whitney. I'm sure that Jeremy will be in touch with you personally once he's out of the hospital."

Reed took her fingers in his but kept her hand captive when she would have withdrawn it. "Not so fast . . . Jennifer, is it? We still have some unfinished business."

"I can't imagine what."

"I need an assistant, that's what. But there's

no point in standing here in the lobby and discussing it. I'd suggest having lunch by the pool except that you need some rest."

His proclamation instantly demolished her own half-resolved intention to take a short nap. "Sorry—I'm going downtown to look through the shops before they close for the long lunch hour. After that, I've planned a ride in a bullock cart and an excursion to the public market. It's just as well," she continued airily. "I wouldn't be of any help to you in selecting an assistant. Jeremy's work is Greek to me—he's the only one in our family with a scientific mind."

Reed didn't move an inch. "That may be, but there's a little matter of a contract. You *do* understand legal obligations?"

Her fingers tightened nervously on the strap of her leather shoulder bag. "Yes, of course. But Dr. Whitney . . ."

"My name's Reed," he interposed smoothly. "There's no need to be so formal."

She stared up at his tall figure in bewilderment. "One minute you're threatening to sue my brother and the next you're telling me there's no need to be formal. I simply don't understand."

"I'd intended to explain it more fully over lunch, but considering that busy schedule of yours, maybe we'd better make it dinner. You do intend to eat dinner?" The last was tacked on with some irony.

"Of course." Her chin went up defiantly.

"The desk clerk has already arranged for my evening."

His brows drew together. "What's that supposed to mean?"

"Just that he recommended a wonderful place to eat in a place called Canico. It's a few miles out of Funchal."

"I was going to suggest the dining room here at the hotel."

"That's just like home," she said scornfully. "It's more fun to get the real flavor of a place when you travel."

"I've had my share of flavor in Africa these past weeks . . ." he began, and then broke off resignedly. "Never mind. We'll try this place if you've made a reservation. Can the hotel clerk manage to fit another paying customer in?"

She looked uncertain. "I suppose so. Do you really want to go along?"

"Unless I waylay you en route to the airport tomorrow, it seems to be my only chance to talk to you. What time do you want to leave for dinner?"

"I don't know—"

"Make it seven-thirty, here in the lobby. I'll arrange for transportation later. Right now I'm going for a swim and having lunch by the pool."

That program sounded so inviting that Jennifer almost weakened, but there was no way without sacrificing her pride in the process. She managed to smile as she said, "And I'm off exploring. Do I need to dress formally for dinner?"

"If it's the kind of place I suspect, you could wear a turtleneck and jeans." He started toward the elevators. "I'll see you down here at seven-thirty—if you're still able to navigate by then."

His last comment acted as a spur every time Jennifer started to weaken during that warm afternoon in Funchal. As she toured the downtown area, the midday heat beat down on the black-and-white mosaic sidewalks and made her clothes cling to her body. Even the brown-and-white oxen hitched to the brightly painted bullock cart she hired on the waterfront gave her an accusing look when they had to move from the shade of a jacaranda tree out into the sunny streets. The breeze that had been blowing at the top of the mountain in the morning became a mere memory, and the humidity next to *Rua del Mar* where the harbor boats docked settled like a wet shroud around her shoulders.

A vision of that gorgeous emerald-green swimming pool at the hotel beckoned like a Lorelei, but Jennifer gritted her teeth and told the boy driving the bullocks to stop at the cathedral so she could see the Moorish cedarwood ceiling. The next stop was a nearby flower market where she ignored the heat as she admired pale pink and green spray orchids along with brilliantly colored bird-of-paradise flowers and anthuriums. They were all so beautiful that she couldn't decide between them and finally emerged clutching a mixed bouquet that would have cost a fortune at home but was a rare bargain in Funchal.

When she'd finished making the rounds of the embroidery shops and wickerwork displays, she was wishing she'd hired the bullock cart for the entire afternoon because every Funchal taxi seemed to be occupied by a Portuguese who knew better than to stand on a stifling street corner clutching an armful of flowers and bulky packages.

By the time Jennifer finally arrived back at the hotel, there was only a half hour to get ready before she met Reed. The floor maid consented to find a vase for the flowers, but there was no one to magically whisk away her aching feet and offer a new pair in their place. A fast glance in the mirror reflected a face without a vestige of color except where the sun had caught the tip of her nose. "Just like an airplane beacon," Jennifer thought disconsolately as she applied powder for the third time. Her gaze wandered over her ivory silk dress with its emerald tie and she decided eight hours of sleep would have been more flattering. As she picked up her tiny straw bag, she had time to notice the last loungers leaving the swimming pool below her hotel window. Their murmured laughter and slow progress toward the cabañas showed that an afternoon by the pool had been highly satisfactory.

The relaxed expression on Reed's face as he waited by the lobby door told the same story when she emerged from the elevator a little later. He looked well groomed and completely at ease in a lightweight gray suit and white shirt. Her second glance showed that his good humor stemmed from the conversation he was holding with a Nordic-looking blonde whose tanned beauty was magnificently set off by the scarlet caftan she was wearing. As Reed noticed Jennifer lingering uncertainly by the reception desk, he said something to the other woman that made her dissolve into laughter before he strode across the lobby.

"I didn't mean to interrupt anything," Jennifer said stiffly when he reached her side.

"You didn't." He took her elbow and started steering her toward the revolving door. "She's just somebody I met at the pool this afternoon."

Jennifer managed a final look at the woman, who was heading slowly toward the hotel's dining room. If the blonde looked that good in a caftan, she must have been a knockout in a bikini earlier. "I thought she might be your wife," Jennifer said casually to the man beside her while they waited for the doorman to flag down a taxi on the busy marine drive which fronted the hotel.

Reed looked amused. "I thought your brother would have mentioned that I wasn't married. We discussed taking wives on field trips when I interviewed him."

"The subject didn't ever come up," Jennifer said hastily.

"I can believe it. From the way you talked at the top of the mountain this morning, I gathered that you didn't have time to fit anything that wore trousers into your schedule. Did you work your way through all the tourist spots on Madeira this afternoon?" His tone showed that his blonde in the caftan clearly hadn't bothered with such trivia.

"Most of them." Fortunately, just then the doorman came running back with a taxi idling behind him so the discussion was momentarily shelved. Another thought suddenly occurred to her instead. "Oh, lord, I forgot to ask the desk clerk for the address of the restaurant," she said, pulling back from the open door of the cab. "I'd better go find out."

"Relax, it's all taken care of," Reed said before she'd managed to take a step. "We'd better hurry up and get started . . . it's a ways out of town."

The taxidriver's command of English was miniscule, but he clearly understood the words "hurry up" and did his best to comply. He wasn't able to get up much speed going through the city center where the merchants were still closing their small shops, but when he finally passed the business district and reached the eastern coastal road which wound upward from the harbor, all of his *Gran Prix* instincts took hold. Each hairpin turn was a challenge and other compact cars merely something to be passed as quickly as possible. Often this was accomplished on the straight-of-way, but a blind curve added zest to his work.

Even Reed tensed at a near miss when they were almost a thousand feet above sea level on the narrow road. He leaned forward and rattled off some biting words in Spanish which were apparently close enough to the driver's Portuguese for the other to lighten his pressure on the accelerator.

Reed sat back and touched Jennifer's wrist. "It's all right now. You can open your eyes," he said.

"Thank you," she murmured faintly as she did. The panorama of the sheer drop down to the sea from her side of the taxi made her catch her breath, and she turned to stare steadily the other way.

"That harbor view is one of the world-famous sights of Madeira, too," Reed said drily. Then he seemed to grasp that she wasn't pretending and he put his hand over her clenched one on the vinyl seat. "Hey, it's all right. These fellows know what they're doing. Actually, this one's a good driver."

She had to swallow before she could reply. "I suppose you're right. It would be nice if they had a guard rail, though. It's at times like this that I wonder why in the world I ever left home."

"I thought you knew about the road when you suggested this place to eat." He glanced at his watch. "It's a little late to make reservations at any other restaurant.

"I'll be all right. Besides, the road's heading inland now so maybe the worst part is over."

"We'll be off the cliff at least," Reed confirmed. "I wish I thought that the restaurant would be an improvement. It sounds like a real tourist trap to me."

"But the man on the desk said that it was wonderful. I thought it would be fun to get away from the tourist fare at the hotels—their menus are just like eating out at home. I found some wonderful little offbeat places in Paris."

He patted her fingers absently. "It's a nice idea, but you have to know what you're doing. Elena said this place was terrible."

Jennifer ignored the last part of his sentence. "Who's Elena?"

"The girl at the pool. She's an airline stewardess who's been vacationing for a couple of weeks."

"I see."

Jennifer's doleful response must have gotten through to Reed because he added in a more bracing tone, "Maybe she's wrong. You might have uncovered a real treasure. I'd just feel better if the place wasn't owned by that desk clerk's brother-in-law."

A little later, when they drove up to a weatherbeaten stucco restaurant set back in a garden where roses and geraniums struggled with the weeds, it became apparent that Elena wasn't far wrong.

The main part of the dining room had pine paneling, dingy tablecloths, and only one other group of paying customers—a table of men in one corner. In another corner, a guitarist and a piano player were struggling to reach the bottom of the sheet music at the same time.

Reed and Jennifer studied the menu in silence, not even commenting on the English translation which proclaimed that the chef served "Foul—all kinds." Finally Reed said, "I'd try the fish—that's usually good. Most restaurants serve the morning's catch. We'll have some wine first—that should improve your morale."

"What about your morale?" she asked before the waiter approached.

"Ask me again in an hour," Reed said, wincing as the pianist hit a sour chord. "There's only one way to go."

After that, things did improve. Jennifer suspected that the generous glass of madeira did its part. She relaxed in its warm glow and discovered she could view the taxi ride back with resignation if not equanimity. When she took another swallow she was even able to laugh as the pianist started a new piece of music.

Reed was watching her more closely than she imagined. "*Now* what?" he wanted to know.

"That tune . . ." she broke off in the middle of a giggle. "I thought it was only heard in English music halls."

He cocked his head to listen. "I don't recognize the melody. That doesn't mean much, though—I'm out of touch with the top twenty."

"That hasn't been in the top twenty for a good seventy years." She picked up her wine glass and offered it in a silent toast, her eyes sparkling. "In Queen Victoria's reign or somewhere around there, I understand it was all the rage. It's 'Have a Little Madeira, Ma' Dear.' "

"I think you've had enough to drink until we get some food. That wine's stronger than you think."

"Don't be silly—that's the title of the song," she protested when he would have taken her glass.

"What is?"

" 'Have a Little Madeira, Ma' Dear.' " Her indignant pronouncement was marred by a slight hiccup in the middle. She frowned slightly. "Maybe it's because I missed lunch."

He reached over then and firmly took the wine glass from her unresisting fingers. "Why in the devil didn't you say so," he muttered, beckoning to the hovering waiter. "I'm surprised that brother of yours lets you out alone."

Jennifer would have been more indignant if a sudden twinge of dizziness hadn't made it an effort to hold her head upright. Only Reed's sharp appraisal kept her in her seat.

"Eat some of that fish," he commanded when a plate was slid in front of her.

She picked up her fork automatically. "I don't really want any. All I want is to lie down." When firm fingers closed over hers, she found herself being fed forcibly. She swallowed a bite in surprise and tried to protest again. "This is ridiculous."

"It is, isn't it." He made her take another bite before releasing his grasp and picking up his own fork. "I'm glad to see that you know how to follow orders occasionally. It's the first thing I require of people who work with me. I insist they eat sensibly and get enough rest. There simply isn't time to get sick and take to your bed when you're traveling around. Besides, most of the beds are damned uncomfortable."

Jennifer had recovered enough to defend herself. "I'm sorry," she said, trying for some dignity. "Normally I don't have any trouble at all."

Surprisingly he didn't quarrel with that. "I know. Your brother said the same thing. I phoned him this afternoon," he went on when her eyes widened in surprise. "It seemed the least I could do. Incidentally, he's coming along fine. I talked to the floor nurse afterward."

"It was kind of you to bother," she began when he cut her off with some amusement.

"I'm never kind. Jeremy will tell you that. Unfortunately, that's the risk of signing a foundation contract." Reed reached for the salt and sprinkled some on his fish before taking another bite.

Jennifer frowned when he didn't go on. "I don't understand. Jeremy couldn't help an appendicitis attack."

"That wasn't what he said this afternoon. He admitted it was a chronic condition," Reed said dispassionately, reaching for a roll. "Now it's too late for me to try and find someone else. I told Jeremy that I'd do my best with his professors when we get back to New York, but I'm afraid that he'll have to choose another slant for his thesis."

"But he's been working for two years on this," she wailed. "He can't afford to throw all that effort out the window. There must be something you can do." She looked across the tablecloth at him hopefully.

As she waited for his answer, the pianist in the corner of the room shuffled his stack of music and started through another fumbling rendition of "Stardust," but his maneuver was ignored by everyone, including the guitarist playing alongside.

Reed kept his attention on his plate as he neatly removed a fish bone and then added some lemon juice to the remaining fillet. "I did make a suggestion to Jeremy that might solve the problem," he said at length. "It's certainly not what I'd choose, but it would salvage his thesis efforts."

"What kind of a suggestion?" she urged impatiently after another pause.

"A makeshift assistant." There was no hesitation to his words now, but he hadn't lost his dispassionate tone. "As I said, it isn't ideal—although things might work out."

"But you said that it was too late to start interviewing candidates over here."

"Much too late. I'm due in Malta two days from now."

"Then it would have to be someone on the spot." Absently she took another swallow of wine. "But there isn't anyone."

"But there is," he interrupted calmly. "Jeremy thought of it. It wouldn't have occurred to me." He placed his knife and fork carefully on the edge of the plate as the pianist lurched into "Red Sails in the Sunset" and the guitarist reached for his wine glass.

Jennifer brushed the hair back from her face and stared across at Reed with a growing sense of foreboding. "You can't mean me," she said finally and waited for his denial.

It didn't come. Instead, he scrutinized her quizzically and said, "I'm afraid so. Jeremy promised that he'd take care of changing your travel arrangements and notify your employer. I don't pretend that it's the ideal solution."

Jennifer wondered how she could have ever thought of him as an absent-minded professor.

Just then there wasn't a thing that escaped that sweeping dark-eyed glance of his. She sat up straighter. "You've ignored one tiny item. Jeremy had no right to make any plans for me. Anyway, the idea of taking another job on my vacation is utterly preposterous!"

"I couldn't agree more. However, it is a way of salvaging your twin's reputation. The only way, I'm afraid." Reed bunched his napkin and put it on the table with finality. "Therefore, if I'm willing to go along with the idea—you certainly should be."

The derision in his tone was scarcely veiled. Jennifer flushed and wilted under it as he obviously knew she would. She watched him pick up the dinner check before he said, "I'll meet you on Malta later this week. Your plane reservation will be ready tomorrow along with an advance on your salary. You can pick them up when you check out."

"That isn't necessary," she tried to say, only to have him continue with his instructions without paying the slightest heed.

"You'll need a typewriter for the reports I'll be dictating. Jeremy said you typed." The last came out in a terse question.

"Yes, I type. What else did Jeremy tell you about me?"

"Nothing at all." Reed seemed genuinely surprised. "I didn't ask. Frankly, I thought I'd find out all I needed to know quite soon enough."

Chapter Two

It was four days later when the plane bearing Jennifer to the island of Malta banked on its final approach to the airport serving the capital city of Valletta. Even if she hadn't been carrying a brand-new portable typewriter and last-minute data from her brother to Reed Whitney, the bleak countryside below would have made her realize that her conventional European holiday had been replaced by a different kind of adventure.

The landing strip was a gray ribbon cutting through acres of flat rocky land in amazing contrast to the French landscape she'd noticed on her drive to Orly airport earlier that day. Jennifer had seen her brother safely on a nonstop flight to New York before she'd started her own journey south to Rome with a final transfer onto a smaller plane which had headed straight over the blue waters of the Mediterranean.

An obliging stewardess had informed her that Malta was approximately sixty miles south of Sicily, but that bare observation hadn't prepared Jennifer for her first glimpse of the rock-ribbed fortress of islands jutting upward from the clear waters around them. Belatedly then, snatches of her history lessons came back; a history that started with the Phoenicians, worked on to Roman emperors and Arabs who eventually gave way to the Spaniards and the great siege with the Turks. But there had been nothing in the text to prepare her for the desolation of the land below her now. While she hadn't expected the modern-day bustle of France nor the lush green hillsides she'd found on Madeira earlier in the week, neither had she expected a locale which looked suspiciously like Alcatraz without the redeeming features of San Francisco just across the Bay.

It was true that the main island of Malta couldn't be described as abandoned; when the plane banked again, she could easily count four cruise ships anchored in what appeared to be the main harbor and small cars whizzed along the narrow roadways crisscrossing the island.

But there was no denying that the overall impression of the place was bleak and unyielding. It resembled her last glimpse of Reed Whitney's countenance when he'd taken her back to the hotel in Madeira that night and peremptorily ordered her to bed. By that time, sheer exhaustion had made her happy to comply. When she awoke the next morning, she found that Dr. Whitney had checked out, leaving behind only her airplane ticket and a check. She'd been tempted to tear up the latter but decided to wait until she'd figured out a scathing reply to go with the scattered pieces. By then, Reed would have learned that she was accompanying him simply as a favor to Jeremy and that her services weren't for sale.

That firm decision had buoyed her in the intervening days, but it only took the first appearance of Malta's rocky coastline to make Jennifer's insides lurch uncomfortably—a sensation that had nothing to do with the *croissant* and *cappuccino* she'd hastily consumed between planes. If it had been Jeremy down below waiting for her arrival, the barren landscape wouldn't have bothered her, but the truth of the matter was that a strange country housing Reed Whitney frankly terrified her.

Her encounters with the male sex in the past hadn't prepared her for a man who had shown no interest whatsoever in her physical assets; instead he'd treated her like an *enfant terrible* plaguing the countryside. Apparently, he'd even imparted his misgivings to Jeremy, because her brother's last words had been, "For pete's sake, Jenny—mind your manners with Reed. I need his cooperation to get those project figures after he's finished. Do as he says and curb those harebrained impulses of yours."

"Wait a minute—I'm not going into indentured slavery even for your sake," she'd protested. "Your precious Dr. Whitney is still in the dark ages where women employees are concerned."

"Don't be an idiot. He's worked with women

ever since he's been with the Foundation. Why, he could have had his pick of the crop, I understand, if he'd even crooked a finger."

"Some women keep cobras for pets, too. There's absolutely no accounting for tastes."

"Well, this time remember you're standing in for me and my thesis. And there's no use looking at me like that." He'd gauged her irritated countenance with remarkable accuracy, considering his weakened state. "You can't hit a man when he's under a doctor's care."

That had made her smile at him reluctantly and bend forward to give him a light kiss on the cheek. "In that case, I'll just have to wait until I get back to New York and you're completely well again."

His grin was almost back to normal. "I'll remember. Send me a postcard from Malta and give my regards to Reed when you see him."

The latter request wasn't as easy to deliver as it sounded. When Jennifer finally went down the airplane steps at the terminal, her quick glance around showed that there was the usual cluster of people to greet new arrivals but no sign of a tall, dark-haired figure among them. She stood in the customs line trying to ignore the temperature that felt more like midsummer than early May. When she was clear of entrance formalities, she waited nervously with her typewriter case in her hands and her suitcases by her side. A minute later, a small, dark-haired man in a lavender shirt sidled up to her. "Miss Rogers?"

Since the top of his head came only to her eye-level, Jennifer looked down in surprise. "I'm Jennifer Rogers."

His darkly tanned face registered relief. "That is good. My name is Elias. Dr. Whitney told me to come meet your plane. I will take your bags to the car." He swept them up as he spoke, his wiry strength belying his lack of inches. "Let me assist you with that, too," he insisted, reaching for her typewriter.

"No, thanks. It isn't heavy." She was looking around confusedly. "Is Dr. Whitney somewhere in the terminal?"

"You mean this building? No, he's at the hotel. If you'll please to follow me. My car is parked through here."

She hurried behind him to the parking area, where he stopped beside an ancient little car with taxi markings on the door. He struggled to unlock the trunk and when he finally managed to undo it, he reached for the typewriter case she was still clutching.

"I'll keep this with me" she said hastily, guarding against possible catastrophe if she let it out of her grasp. The fact that her tweed luggage was going to be covered with Maltese dust was unimportant as long as Reed's property emerged unscathed.

"As you wish, Miss Rogers, but there's no need to worry." Elias pulled up the trunk lid with a negligent gesture and started to deposit her larger bag inside. He'd barely gotten it halfway in when he gave a convulsive start and his mocha skin turned almost gray.

As he stood there motionless, staring into the trunk, Jennifer moved forward in alarm. "What is it, Elias? Is something wrong?" Her gaze swept swiftly over the interior where a bald spare tire was shoved into one corner next to a package about the size of a car battery which was securely wrapped in black plastic. There was nothing to excite any suspicion and she turned back to the stricken driver. "Aren't you feeling well? I'll get some help."

"No . . . no." His free hand shot out to stop her. "I'm sorry, Miss Rogers. I just remembered an errand—something I should have delivered before I met you." He put her suitcase back on the ground and closed the trunk carefully. "It would be better for you to go in another car."

Jennifer frowned as her glance swept the deserted parking lot around them. "Where do I find one? They must have all gone into town."

"Another taxi will come sometime," he announced.

He would have carried her bags back toward the terminal if Jennifer hadn't stayed stubbornly where she was. "Now look here, Elias," she said with the determination of a traveler who isn't going to relinquish the only cab in sight, "I don't want to wait around for another car. Dr. Whitney paid you to deliver me to the hotel, didn't he?"

"Yes . . . but I could give back the money." He reached reluctantly toward a grimy shirt pocket.

"Keep the money," she said, and then tried appealing to another side of his nature. "Look— it's very warm and I'm tired. I don't even mind if you make your delivery on the way to my hotel—just so long as I get there eventually."

His thin face took on a shuttered look. "I cannot do that."

"Why not? I promise not to tell Dr. Whitney about any of this. Actually, I don't mind a little sightseeing before you drop me off," she said, trying to sound like an eager tourist. "This is my first visit to Malta and I won't be here very long." She could see him wavering and walked around to open the taxi door. "Just shove my bags in the trunk and let's get going."

For a second it seemed as if the thin driver was going to hold out against her blandishments—then his resistance collapsed. Either the thought of refunding Reed's stipend or the suffocating heat got to him. It could even have been the sight of Jennifer climbing determinedly into the back seat of his cab. At any rate, he simply heaved a troubled sigh and muttered, "I'll put your suitcases in the front seat. It is better that way. The trunk is not clean enough."

By then, Jennifer wouldn't have objected if

he'd tied them on the roof. "Whatever you say," she said happily and sat back as he stowed her luggage next to the driver's seat and then went to get behind the wheel. He took time for a sweeping look around the parking lot before starting the engine and pulling carefully away from the curb. "I will drive slowly, Miss Rogers," he announced. "Many times the tourists have complained about the traffic danger here on the island. We have many cars and our roads are narrow."

"Whatever you say," Jennifer said in some bewilderment. Elias had seemed so reluctant to take her that she'd been prepared to be delivered unceremoniously after one of the faster trips on record. Reed must have put the whammy on him, she decided, as they tooled out of the airport onto a main road with a speed more fitting to a funeral hearse than a taxi. After the first half mile of such circumspect driving, Jennifer leaned back in the seat and decided to enjoy it. At this rate, Elias could deliver packages all day if he wanted to.

She could see the buildings of Valletta in the distance, but noticed that Elias turned away from them at the first roundabout in the road, which apparently was one of the lingering features of British heritage on the island. Other remnants were the English-style lorries which made up most of the traffic with their trailer loads of potatoes and onions.

"We export these two vegetables," Elias said,

noting her interest. "We don't have many things to export," he went on bitterly. "Even now, many of our people have to go abroad to make a living."

Jennifer was reluctant to get in the middle of a political argument. "I was just thinking how prosperous everything looked," she said, gesturing toward the neat yellow limestone buildings lining the suburban street they were passing through. The cobblestone thoroughfare was thronged with children carrying satchels on the way home for the midday break, children looking as polished and clean in their school uniforms as the gleaming brass dolphin doorknockers found on every house along the street. Up on the tile roofs of the dwellings, a solid network of television antennas could be seen.

Elias waved a disparaging hand. "Here, maybe. But not in other parts of the island. Living conditions are very bad—like the street surface." He drove carefully around some road-repair signs marking an area where cobblestones had been removed and stagnant water stood in the gap. "It has been like that for months. There are even mosquitoes causing disease from such a place," Elias said, when the traffic had sorted itself out again and he'd resumed his steady twenty-mile-per-hour speed. "Of course, you won't have such problems out at the Hilton. No foreigners would live in such

conditions. They would not tolerate this ineffi-
ciency."

"Are there many foreigners living on Malta?"
she asked in honest curiosity. "I thought most
of them had gone home once the islands became independent."

"There's still a small British garrison, but
only until our treaty agreement finishes. There
are many Americans here, though."

"Visitors?"

He kept his attention on the road, which was
narrowing as they drove farther into the barren
countryside. "Not visitors. These are oil men
working in Libya and all around the Mediterranean while their families live here. Oil exploration is a big business. You will see what I
mean."

By then, Jennifer was thoroughly confused.
The rock-strewn landscape around them was
almost flat and looked like the remnant of a
gigantic gravel bed. Small landholdings were
marked out with waist-high stone fences and
often prickly pear cactus appeared to be the
only crop thriving on the thin soil. Her eyes
widened a moment later when she saw a man
carrying a shotgun as he stalked through a
field.

She leaned forward to get Elias's attention.
"What's going on? There isn't any guerrilla
warfare here, is there?" As he glanced back
uncomprehendingly, she gestured behind them.
"That man with the gun."

The car swerved dangerously. "What man? Where?"

She clutched the upholstery to keep her balance. "The one we just passed back on that last farm. There were shotgun shells all over his vest."

"Oh, that." Elias' thin shoulders relaxed. "He's hunting pigeons. Most of the men do it in their spare time." He braked as they came around a turn and found the highway blocked by a flock of goats. An old woman was trying to herd them onto the side of the road and Elias gave an exclamation of annoyance at the delay.

"It's all right," Jennifer assured him. "I'm enjoying it. It's a pity that I left my camera in my suitcase," she went on, smiling at the goats' refusal to be hurried.

Elias didn't offer to pull over so that she could unearth it. "Dr. Whitney won't be pleased," he muttered. Then he gave an exclamation of relief as the roadway cleared and drove on past with his horn blaring.

A few minutes later, the highway circled a picturesque cove denting the island's coastline. Some gaily painted *dghajjes*, the distinctive Maltese dinghies, were moored near the shore, but Jennifer's attention was taken by a towering piece of machinery on a platform anchored near the middle of the bay.

"What in the world is that?" she asked Elias.

"An oil-drilling rig that's been brought here for repairs. That was what I was telling you about," he commented sourly. "All run by foreigners off our shores."

"I didn't realize there was any oil around here," she said.

"Most of the work is being done off the Libyan coast, but we hope they will find favorable discoveries near Malta. Then the island's fortunes will change. We'll be as powerful as some others in this part of the world."

Jennifer was beginning to realize that it took very little for Elias to mount his national soapbox. She thought he was too intent on his oratory to be concerned with his driving, but he surprised her a moment later by slowing to turn off the road onto a dirt track which wound down to a stone fortress on the very edge of the cliff. "Where are we going now?" she asked in some alarm.

He hesitated for a moment before replying, shifting into a lower gear when the rutted track ran out altogether. A few feet more and he braked almost in the shadow of the ruin.

"This is one of the old Moorish towers," he explained after he'd turned off the ignition. "They were part of the fortifications when our ancestors had to defend themselves against the invaders."

"I see." Jennifer surveyed the crumbling limestone structure with interest. "And what do they use them for now?"

"Nothing special." Elias was opening his

door as he spoke. "There is something I must deliver. It won't take long."

A moment later she heard the trunk lid open and then slam down again. Elias reappeared, this time carefully carrying the small plastic-wrapped package from the trunk against his chest.

Jennifer started to get out of the car. "I think I'll see if I can get a picture from the top of the cliff. The edge of the tower would make a wonderful frame on one side with the sea beyond."

"No!" Elias snapped out the word sharply. When he saw her astonished expression, he softened his tone. "Strangers are not allowed next to the tower. This is land that belongs to the government."

Jennifer frowned and looked at the knee-high weeds surrounding the limestone battlement. "They certainly don't take very good care of it. Besides," she added defensively, "you're walking around. What's the difference?"

"Please, Miss Rogers, get back in the car." Elias abandoned his attempt to emulate official-dom and just sounded like a frightened young man. He looked like one, too, as he checked to see if anyone was watching their exchange. His air of alarm was strong enough that Jennifer followed his glance, but there was nothing she could see other than the deserted ruin whose outlines had been weathered through the ages. A moment later, when a cloud dimmed the sun, the old fortification took on a foreboding cast, heightened by the weed-strewn field around it and the shadowed gray Mediterranean waves striking the cliffside far below.

Jennifer shivered and was retreating back into the car when she heard the noise of another automobile nearby. She glanced up the hillside and saw an expensive-looking gray car being turned onto the main road before it disappeared back toward Valletta.

She leaned forward to see if Elias had heard the disturbance, but he was almost out of sight at the bottom of the abandoned tower. When he reappeared minutes later and came striding back toward the car, he looked like a young man without a worry in the world. Overhead, the sun emerged from its veiling of clouds and Jennifer gave herself a mental shake. She'd flown too far and slept too little—that was the trouble.

Her voice was light and uncaring when Elias got back in the car. "Now can we go on to the hotel?"

He sounded equally casual, "Without another stop, Miss Rogers. We should be there within twenty minutes."

A little later, when they were on the road retracing their route, he said diffidently, "Dr. Whitney might be annoyed that you are so late arriving. Perhaps it would be better not to tell him of our small detour. You could always say that the plane was late . . ." he let his voice trail off suggestively. "If you don't mind."

Jennifer frowned. "I doubt if the subject will ever come up, so you needn't worry." Then she added reassuringly. "I enjoyed seeing more of the island. Once I start working for Dr. Whitney, there won't be time for sightseeing."

There was no more discussion after that as they drove rapidly back to the more populated part of the island. Apparently Elias had forgotten about his promise to maintain a safe speed limit, and Jennifer had to hang on when he passed a truck loaded with potatoes and barely managed to slither past an oncoming one loaded with machinery parts. Fortunately after that the traffic was forced to slow as they entered the populous Floriana suburb where white-gloved traffic policemen were keeping a strict eye at intersections. Then the road circled colorful St. George's Bay into what was obviously the tourist hotel area of the island.

Bright bowers of red and purple bougainvillea transformed the grounds of the Malta Hilton into a luxurious parklike setting that softened and complemented the contemporary building set on the edge of another cliff overlooking the sea. Elias aimed his car toward the door with a final spurt and then let the taxi coast for the last few feet to save gasoline. "You will remember what we decided about Dr. Whitney," he told Jennifer hastily before the bellman could reach the door handle.

Jennifer nodded and escaped into the refrigerated coolness of the big modern lobby. A mirrored pillar made her aware that the cab ride had done little to improve her appearance; her ivory shirtwaist was still unwrinkled, but the bodice was clinging in a way that the designer had never intended. She ignored the reception clerk's interested masculine gaze and hoped that Reed wouldn't materialize from a far corner.

He still hadn't put in an appearance when she finished registering, nor was there a message waiting for her at the porter's desk. Jennifer felt such a surge of relief that she lingered over an expensive jewelry display in a corner of the lobby before following a bellman to her room.

She was conducted down a long corridor where the windows overlooked a magnificent view of the Mediterranean. Each room had its own lanai, allowing guests a chance to sun in private while admiring the seascape or the colorful pool area directly below.

Jennifer barely had time to note the sleek Scandinavian decor of her room with its contemporary teak furniture before stepping out onto the lanai and taking a deep, contented breath. When Dr. Whitney returned to civilization from his Foundation projects, he did it with a vengeance. Never in her wildest imaginings had she expected to find such five-star comfort in Malta.

A knock on the door did nothing to dim her starry view. She was humming as she went to open it but broke off immediately when she saw her employer's figure in the hall.

His first words showed that he didn't share her cheerful mood. "Where the devil have you been? Elias left here a good two hours ago to pick you up. When I checked with the airline, they said your flight was just ten minutes late in landing."

Jennifer felt a familiar feeling of confusion sweep over her. Every time she came into contact with the man in front of her, she found herself on the defensive. After viewing two hotel maids listening to the exchange, she opened the door wider and motioned him in. "If you don't mind, I'd rather be reprimanded in private." Reed gave her an annoyed look, but he came in and shut the door smartly behind him.

As he walked over to sit on the only upholstered chair, she noticed that he was wearing a casual outfit of cotton slacks and a sport shirt which showed he hadn't spent the morning in a business meeting. A second look revealed that his dark hair was still gleaming with water and her temperature rose even more. Apparently he hadn't met her at the airport because of a previous appointment with the hotel swimming pool. And he had the nerve to criticize when she reported a little late!

"Naturally I feel a responsibility toward anyone who works for me," he said, starting again. "When you didn't arrive, I was afraid something had happened. I was even about to call the Embassy and see if any accidents had been reported. Elias drives like a bat out of hell most of the time, and it's a miracle that his car even runs." Reed broke off to eye her carefully. "You're still in one piece, though, so it couldn't have been car trouble."

"You're right about that." Jennifer realized that he wasn't going to be fobbed off with a feeble excuse, but she wanted one question settled first. "Why did you send him to meet me in the first place if he has so many shortcomings?"

Reed winced visibly. "I thought you'd get around to that sooner or later. There was a call from the Egyptian Embassy about your visa application this morning and I had to appear in person to settle it. After I'd explained the last-minute rush, they agreed to let you come with the rest of us."

Jennifer absently brushed her hair back from her warm face. "What do you mean by 'the rest of us'? I thought this was your project, with only Jeremy to assist you."

Reed's stern jaw relaxed. "I can see you haven't been connected with many Foundation grants. The board of directors extol international cooperation, whether it's the most efficient method or not. That way, no individual reaps all the glory or the sour grapes. In this case, there's an official Foundation group, but we work independently. I wanted you to meet the rest earlier, but . . ." His broad shoulders lifted in a careless shrug.

"I'm sorry." She began to understand his concern.

"Well, don't look so stricken. I didn't mean to bite your head off, but I had visions of explaining to Jeremy how you'd become a traffic statistic on Malta before you even started work."

"Plus the annoyance of having to hire another typist."

Reed kept his tone just as solemn as hers. "A hell of a nuisance." He shifted his tall frame in the chair. "You still haven't said what happened."

"I'm not sure myself." She moved over to the lanai door and then turned to face him. "Elias met me right on schedule and we were ready to come straight to the hotel when suddenly he muttered something about a delivery he had to make at the other end of the island."

"Why didn't you get another cab?"

"They'd all left by that time, and the only people I'd heard in the terminal were speaking a language that was Greek to me."

"You're wrong there—it was probably Maltese."

"It might as well have been ancient Babylonian," she insisted. "I didn't understand a word of it."

"That's not surprising. Maltese is about seventy-five-percent Arabic, twenty-percent Italian, and five-percent Spanish."

"Well, it left me one-hundred-percent confused," she admitted. "Elias was a lifeline I didn't want to abandon. He wasn't keen to take me with him on his errand."

"Probably because I'd told him to deliver you straight here and to drive carefully on the way."

"That could be it, although I got the feeling that he really didn't want me along. It's a funny thing . . ."

"What is?"

"Elias wasn't consistent at all. He drove like he was carrying crates of eggs when we started out, but on the way back he set a new speed record." The memory of that close call with the truck made her shudder visibly.

Reed scowled as he noted her distress. "Then I come along and complete the morning by snarling at you."

Jennifer found herself more distracted by his unspoken apology than his anger. "My brother could tell you that I don't melt and I can take care of myself very well."

"So I noticed—in Madeira."

A flush suffused her cheekbones. "That's not fair."

"No, it wasn't." Reed got up but lingered by his chair. "Jeremy also could tell you that I don't always follow the rules, but you'll find that out by yourself in the next week or so. Now you'd better get changed."

"I can be ready in half an hour," she told

him briskly as she followed him to the door. "What's next on the agenda?"

"That's up to you. I have one more appointment, but there's no reason why that should interfere with your sightseeing. You've never been to Malta before, have you?"

She shook her head. "To be honest, I had to look in an atlas to find it before I came here. I just knew it was somewhere in the Mediterranean. Is it a hobby of yours to go from island to island?"

Reed paused with his hand on the doorknob. "Not especially. Madeira was my idea for a few days off; Malta is part of the work schedule. The desalinization plant here has helped the economy, but not enough. In the meantime, oil prices have put a crimp in the treasury and Malta's trying to recover by exploring for oil on their own offshore shelf."

Her expression lightened. "I saw an oil rig in for repairs at a place called Pretty Bay. Elias was bitter that foreigners were in charge of the exploration project."

"The politicians have been busy on all sides," Reed commented wryly.

"But how do you fit into it all?"

"Only on the fringes. The government's aware that their fishing industry could be endangered if something like that blowout on the North Sea happened here. The Foundation has been called on to assess the potential dangers of exploratory drilling and recommend what precautions should be taken. Since I was in the area, they asked me to come and add my two cents' worth. There's a dull report you can type when you have time, but there'll be an opportunity on the boat."

"Wait a minute." Jennifer stopped him halfway over the threshold. "Did you say 'boat'?"

"That's right. The one we're taking to Egypt. It sails tomorrow night. Any objection?"

"I guess not . . . I mean . . ." She swallowed and started over again. "You didn't mention anything about a ship going to Egypt."

"We have to get there somehow," Reed said brusquely, looking at his watch. "That's why you'd better get cracking if you plan to see anything of Malta. There's still time for you to have a swim before lunch. I'll meet you down by the pool in twenty minutes if that sounds good."

By then, Jennifer was past protesting even if she'd been inclined. "It sounds fine. You don't have to go in again, though—just to keep me company."

He looked puzzled. "I don't know what you're talking about. I haven't beeen swimming."

"But your hair was wet . . ." she broke off in embarrassment at his suddenly mocking expression.

"I'd just gotten out of the shower after coming back from the Embassy hassle. So that's why you were so annoyed—you thought I was

cavorting in the swimming pool all morning."
He shook his head. "The workings of the female
mind!"

There was no use trying to explain, Jennifer
decided. Especially since he had read her
thoughts with such unerring accuracy. She
moved pointedly over to her suitcases. "It's a
good thing I threw in a swimsuit at the last
minute. Twenty minutes should be just about
right." She ignored the muffled chuckle which
was Reed's only response and didn't look up
again until the door had closed behind him.

When she went down the terrace steps to the
swimming pool a little later, she lingered to admire the display of ivy geraniums cascading
from some big terracotta containers. The scarlet
blooms were just one facet of the color around
her; bright green lounges and umbrella tables
at the poolside added another as hotel guests
enjoyed their leisure. The long salt-water pool
with its blue-tiled finish beckoned like an oasis
in the midday heat.

Jennifer didn't linger any longer; she slid out
of her flowered nylon robe and left it on an
empty chair, pulling on her swim cap as she
walked toward the pool's edge. A moment later,
she gave a gasp of pleasure as she dived into
the cool depths of the water. She had stroked
her way across the center and was happily
floating on her back when Reed's powerful
form surfaced beside her.

For a moment she could only stare at him,

amazed at how the angular planes of his face relaxed as he treaded water effortlessly. Without his horn-rimmed glasses and stern professorial air, he looked five years younger. She managed to move her glance away from the broad expanse of tanned shoulders and chest so close to her, but the effort showed in her breathless tone. "You startled me. Do you make a habit of creeping up on people?"

"Next time I'll jump in and give you advance warning." He shook his head ruefully. "That's what comes from leading such a solitary existence—I forget how to behave around women."

Since Jennifer vividly remembered the look of patent adoration shown by his blonde in Madeira and saw the attention he was getting from two women swimmers, she didn't bother to acknowledge such sheer nonsense. It was all too evident that he'd forgotten more about the feminine sex than most men ever learned.

Reed didn't linger to discuss it. "Come along—the rest of our people are waiting over there to meet you." He jerked his head toward an umbrella table by the shallow end of the pool.

"You mean now?" Jennifer asked, suddenly remembering the brevity of her bikini.

"That's what I had in mind." He sounded puzzled. "Why? What's wrong with that?"

"Nothing," she said hastily. "Just a second until I get my things—they're on the other side of the pool."

"Don't bother. You look okay . . ." Reed broke off when he found that she was already halfway across the pool and was paying no attention. His eyes narrowed as he watched her slim figure come out of the water. She used a towel briefly and then shrugged into her nylon coverup, which discreetly shrouded all her curves. He smiled slightly and pushed off to follow her.

By the time he emerged beside her, she was trying to smooth her damp hair.

"You look fine," he told her, and took a towel offered by a pool attendant to dry his shoulders. "Let's go, shall we?"

In contrast to his relaxed attitude, the three people who watched their approach didn't miss a thing. Edwin Rudolph was the senior member of the group, a man in his early forties with graying hair and a forbidding expression on his lined, thin face that made him look like a figure from an El Greco canvas. The petite blonde woman beside him was about the same age, but she revealed such an effusive manner that Jennifer almost expected to see a badge identifying her as a professional hostess. Instead, Reed introduced her as Louise Sutton, personal secretary to the older man. The final member of the group was Franz Schoman, who was presented as Ed Rudolph's assistant.

"General dogsbody would be closer to it," Franz insisted as he stared appreciatively at Jennifer and held her fingers much longer than a handshake warranted. He was a brown-haired man in his late twenties, with the medium height of a southern European. His waistline showed that he hadn't missed any meals but it didn't lessen his attractiveness because he had an engaging grin and soulful dark eyes. There was the slightest trace of a German accent in his voice, although he managed English without any hesitation. "I've been looking forward to your arrival ever since Reed told us about you," he confessed. "Sit down, won't you? We're about to order lunch."

Jennifer was just moving over to a metal chair on the far side of the table when she felt Reed's hand clamp down on her shoulder.

"I'm sorry," he told them, "but I'm afraid there won't be time. Miss Rogers' plane was late and I have a lot of work for her to get through this afternoon."

Even Ed Rudolph protested at that. "*Gott in Himmel*, Reed, the girl has to eat. I know better than to try tactics like that on my secretary." He looked over at the blonde woman by his side with a self-satisfied smirk and patted her hand.

Louise Sutton acknowledged it with an arch glance and tilted her carefully made-up face so that she was out of the sun. "Ed's right, Reed, darling. Jennifer should get to know us all. Besides, if there's time for both of you to go swimming, there's certainly time to have lunch."

Jennifer wondered how Reed was going to refute that logic, but she needn't have worried. "The swim was therapy for her plane trip," he said to the older woman, keeping his hand firmly on Jennifer's shoulder. "Besides, I promised to order some sandwiches later on if starvation threatens."

"That's ridiculous," Louise protested. "She could sit here in the sun and dry her hair while she's having something to eat with us."

Jennifer felt she'd been discussed long enough. "It really isn't important, Miss Sutton."

"Louise . . . please," the older woman insisted.

"Louise," Jennifer amended with a smile. "Honestly, I'm not a bit hungry."

The blonde woman made a resigned murmur and patted her own carefully coiffed hair. It was clear that she didn't intend to let salt water have a chance to wreck her appearance.

Edwin merely shrugged and reached for a menu. "It's your affair, Whitney. My reports have already been turned in to the Ministry here—Franz delivered them this morning. I presume yours will make the deadline."

"I don't anticipate any difficulty."

Reed's voice was without expression, but both of the other men shot him a quick glance and Edwin hastily said, "Of course, of course. Well, there'll be plenty of time for—Jennifer, is it?—to get acquainted on our crossing to Egypt."

Louise summoned a bright smile at that. "Two days just to relax and have fun. We're all looking forward to it."

There was a pause as they looked at Jennifer. "It sounds very nice," she managed politely.

"Even better now," Franz murmured with evident sincerity.

Reed didn't give her a chance to reply. "We'll see you later then," he announced, shifting his hand down Jennifer's back to nudge her in the direction of the cabañas.

She let him get away with it until they were beyond hearing distance of the others. Then she slowed her pace to give him a severe look. "What in the dickens is going on? Is there really so much to do that there isn't time to eat? You should have told me—I didn't need a swim *that* much."

Reed looked over his shoulder before saying, "Forget it. I filed my report this morning, too. It was the only excuse I could think of for getting away from them. You see, I've arranged for a picnic lunch," he went on hesitantly. "I thought you might like to see some other parts of the island since we won't be here long."

"I'd love a picnic. Are you sure that you want to bother?"

"If I hadn't, I wouldn't have mentioned it in the first place," he replied, sounding more like normal. "I'm not overly fond of our co-workers, and we might as well be on our own while we can. There's no way of escaping once we're on the ship."

Jennifer felt he needn't have been so hasty in pointing out that she was simply the lesser of two evils. For an instant, she was tempted to say that the heat had given her a headache, but then her common sense prevailed. Whatever Reed's reason, a picnic and a chance to sightsee on this fabulous island were two things not to be missed. "I'll hurry getting dressed," she said finally. "Let's hope we get out of the hotel without being caught."

"Don't worry about that. Ed eats every meal as if it's his last supper and Franz is getting the same habit. We should have clear sailing for the next half hour, at least." Reed pulled up at the bathers' entrance to the hotel. "Shall I meet you in the parking lot?"

"That'll be fine. Is Elias driving us?"

"Not if I can help it. I'll have to think of an excuse so we don't hurt his feelings." Seeing her amazed expression, he said, "What's the matter?"

"Nothing . . . really." Despite herself, she felt her cheeks redden. "I just didn't realize that you worried about things like that."

"Only on odd Tuesdays and *never* with my secretaries. So get going, will you!" He gave her derriére a negligent slap with the back of his hand, blandly ignored her surprised gasp, and disappeared into the hotel.

By the time Jennifer had showered and

dressed, she'd used all of the half hour. Finding sunglasses and a scarf cost another five minutes, so she prudently took a service stairway down that didn't go near the pool area. The early afternoon heat of the parking lot made her draw in her breath sharply and she began to understand the reason for the long afternoon siesta period on the island. Then she saw Reed beckoning from the interior of a small dark blue car parked in the shade of a eucalyptus tree and she hurried toward him.

She slid onto the bucket seat next to him and winced as her thigh came into contact with the scorching vinyl.

"Only mad dogs and Englishmen," Reed muttered in apology as he noticed her action. "I should have taken you out after dinner."

"No way," she assured him. "I told Jeremy that I intend to come back from this trip with a fabulous suntan." She inspected Reed's profile as she spoke. "Anybody would think you'd wintered in Palm Springs."

He chuckled and turned on the ignition. "Then I'll keep quiet about my mud hut in central Africa. Did you get out of the hotel without running into the terrible trio?"

"I didn't see a soul." She half-turned in the seat. "Are they really so bad?"

He grinned at that. "Not really—unless you want a quick meal somewhere. When you eat with Ed, everything takes on the trappings of a state banquet. Actually, Louise and Franz are pleasant people—I've just been on my own so long that I get impatient."

Jennifer's eyebrows climbed. "Then I'm surprised that you wanted me along."

Reed took his gaze from the traffic long enough to say, "I thought we'd covered that topic in Madeira." His voice showed that he hadn't altered his original opinion. Picnic or no, she was still only a stopgap for Jeremy.

After that, there was a silence between them for the time it took to skirt the bay next to the casino and edge into Valletta's city traffic.

Reed was the one who finally broke it. "It should be less crowded once we get out in the country. I thought you might enjoy having lunch by the Blue Grotto at the other end of the island."

Jennifer was happy to respond to his overture. "That sounds wonderful! I'm glad you're driving," she confessed. "I didn't realize the Maltese followed English rules."

"Didn't Elias tell you any of the history?"

"I forgot to ask him." A faint frown creased her forehead. "What was his reaction when you said we were going off on our own?"

"He wasn't around the parking lot or the hotel entrance when I looked. You must have frightened him off this morning. I hope he gets back soon because if Ed or Franz want to go out separately this afternoon—there'll be hell to pay. Their Mercedes is the only other official Foundation car," he went on when she looked confused. "This is just a rental I arranged for at the last minute."

She started to laugh. "I see. Do you need a legitimate reason for such tactics?"

"How about a visit to the desalinization plant?"

"Sounds good. Are we going?"

"Nope, but I was there two days ago so I have all my answers ready." His expression was wry. "I'm already acting like a slippery customer. That's what having a woman around does to a man."

"You mean that if Jeremy were here . . ."

"He'd damn well find the Blue Grotto on his own." It was an emphatic statement, but he didn't enlarge on it because in the next breath he was saying, "Did you notice those wrought-iron light fixtures on the street corners?"

"They're beautiful," Jennifer responded, although she was still turning over his last statement in her mind. "I noticed the dolphin doorknockers in this block when Elias was driving me to the hotel. I'd love to take one of those home with me."

"No reason you can't." Reed gave her a quick scrutiny. "You mean Elias toured you down this way?"

"I'm pretty sure we came back on this route, although I didn't see any Blue Grotto. Why?"

"I was just curious. Do you remember any landmarks?"

She had to think before she could say,

"There was that place called Pretty Bay I was telling you about. It was near the tower where he made his delivery. One of those old fortifications they have along the coast."

He gave a silent whistle. "No wonder you were late arriving." Then he added reflectively, "I heard somewhere that all those old towers were abandoned—seems like a funny place to deliver a package."

"I thought that, too, but Elias didn't volunteer any information and I wasn't in the position to ask." Her lips quirked in a small smile. "All I wanted, believe it or not, was to be delivered to my employer in one piece."

"And he was such an ungrateful Scrooge that he took your head off anyway. Maybe lunch will help make up for it."

"If the size of that picnic basket means anything—you're home free. I can't wait to find out what's inside."

"You'll have to, but only about fifteen more minutes." He was accelerating as he spoke.

There was almost no traffic on the road as they approached the south end of the island. The terraced farmlands alongside were the familiar subsistence plots with waist-high rock fences to mark the boundaries. Gray native stone and faded yellow limestone were used for the buildings in the few small villages they passed and the colors did little to brighten the dull, monochromatic surroundings. It took the

bright blue of the Mediterranean to accomplish
that when they finally reached the coast.

"Gorgeous, isn't it?" Jennifer said with a
happy sigh. "What a difference that water
makes."

"Just wait until you see the Blue Grotto,"
Reed promised, driving carefully on the winding road, which had narrowed until two cars
were barely able to pass. "It's not as spectacu-
lar as its namesake in Capri, but a lot less
crowded."

"From the way Elias talked, the Maltese are
busier with politics than trying to attract tourists. That makes for a better picnic," she added
lightly, sitting up straighter as they drove
through a small town. "What are all those
women doing sitting on the steps of that building? They're too quiet for a protest meeting."

He chuckled. "You've been reading the
wrong newspapers. They're just eating their
sack lunches and playing tombola at the same
time. Probably do it every noon."

"Tombola?" Jennifer sounded puzzled as she
stared back at them.

"Bingo—or its British cousin." He was pulling
off the road in a shaded view spot that had obviously been used by picnickers before. "Good!
We have this place all to ourselves. The grotto
is just down there—you'll be able to see it from
where we eat."

Jennifer barely waited until he'd taken the
key from the ignition before she was opening

her door. "This was a wonderful idea! I'll carry that small basket," she offered, reaching into the back of the car.

"Don't bounce it around," Reed cautioned her as he handed it over, before lifting out a larger hamper. "That's the wine and a couple of glasses."

"You *do* go first class," she teased, following him a little way down the hillside until he stopped by a broad, waist-high concrete barrier.

"When in Malta, it doesn't pay to argue with the head waiter. Sit down and relax while I see what we're eating."

She perched on the wall, leaving space enough for the basket between them, and gave a happy sigh as she gazed down at the picturesque scene far below them where the waters of the Mediterranean poured through a mammoth limestone arch. The colors were magnificent, with a phosphorescent glow from the blue subterranean depths and a prism effect caused by the sunlight when the waves dashed against the cliffside at the waterline.

"All this and no people," Jennifer exulted. "Imagine those women back in the town playing bingo when they could eat down here."

"The scenery's old hat to them," Reed said, intent on unpacking the contents of the basket.

"I notice that you're more concerned with calories, too," she teased, laughing.

"I need more than food for my soul at the

moment. It looks as if we have two of everything. Although that doesn't matter if you're
content looking at the scenery."

"I didn't say that." She settled into a more
comfortable position on the wall and surveyed
the packets laid out between them. "What's on
the menu?"

"Syrian bread, Danish cheese, Portuguese
wine, Greek olives, some kind of a Lebanese
pastry that's mostly honey and nuts, and
oranges from Morocco." He eyed her challeng-
ingly. "I hope you're not one of those women
who only eats cottage cheese salads for lunch."

She gave him a pitying glance and reached
for the bread. "You *have* been out of touch.
Uncork the wine, will you? I'll divide the
cheese."

After that there were only snatches of conversation, such as, "Please pass the salt," "How
in the world did honey get in the olives?" and
finally Reed's comment when he emptied the
wine bottle into their glasses, "Might as well
drink it—the waiter at the hotel would think we
were crazy if we brought any back."

It was probably a half hour later before Jennifer stowed the lunch remnants back in the
baskets along with the empty bottle and glasses
and then stretched luxuriously. "I don't know
whether it's the sunshine or the wine or the
combination, but I'd like to sleep for the rest of
the afternoon. No wonder these people take a
siesta."

"From what I've heard about those, sleeping isn't the only activity." Reed stood up and stretched in leisurely fashion himself before taking a picnic basket in each hand. "I'll put these in the car," he added, without altering his tone.

Jennifer stared after him and then made her way slowly back to the car so her flushed cheeks would have time to cool. She stayed determinedly on a safe topic as she remarked, "This outing was a wonderful idea, but now I'm ready to start earning my salary. Probably your work will take me the rest of the afternoon. I'm not a very fast typist."

"There's plenty of time." He walked around to open the car door for her. "Actually I'm curious about the old tower that Elias visited this morning. If it's the one I'm thinking of, it's practically on our way back to Valletta. Let's take a small detour en route." The last was said as he got behind the steering wheel. "It'll give you a chance to take pictures of a couple villages and their fishing fleets. Jeremy will be impressed when you show him."

"That will be a change," she said cheerfully. "Usually I have to rope and tie him before he'll look at any of my vacation pictures."

There was a contented silence between them after that until a little later when Reed indicated a cove ahead of them on the right. "That's the place called Pretty Bay. Does it look familiar?"

She nodded slowly. "I think so. We approached it from the other end, though. The road over there on the top of that cliff. If I'm right, the tower's beyond the bend."

"Sounds plausible." Reed gave her an approving look. "You can navigate for me anytime."

"Wait until we see if I'm right," she cautioned.

He merely grinned at that and didn't say any more as they drove around the attractive cove where the towering oil rig was anchored amid the brightly colored fishing dinghies.

"Now, let's see what's around the bend," Reed said, accelerating again as the road climbed. A moment later he grinned at her crow of triumph. "One tower—as advertised," he confirmed. "Complete with goats in the foreground. You didn't tell me it was furnished with livestock as well."

"It wasn't when we were here before." She hung onto the door handle as he pulled off onto the rough grassy field a few minutes later. "This is almost the same place I saw the other car . . ." she began and then shook her head when his eyebrows went up questioningly. "Nothing important. What are we going to do now?"

He set the brake and switched off the ignition. "Take a walk down to the tower and see if that package of Elias's is still there."

"Should we? He said something about this property belonging to the government."

Reed reached into the back seat to retrieve his camera and started fiddling with the film advance lever. "Those goats won't object to our company, and that herder is sound asleep over there against the wall. If anyone else comes around, we can always say that we're just tourists looking for some pictures. Oh, hell!"

Jennifer paused halfway out the door. "What's the matter?"

"I forgot to change film after that last picture I shot of the Grotto." He leaned over the seat to rummage in his belongings on the floor. "Good, I brought another roll." As he straightened again, he said, "Sorry to hold you up, but I might as well do this in comfort. This model is tricky to load."

"I'll wander on ahead. Maybe I can pet a goat while I'm waiting. Do you suppose they understand English?"

Reed looked amused. "Damned if I know. Ask one and see. If you find a handsome one, tell him to stick around and have his picture taken. I'll be down in a few minutes."

She nodded and gave him a blithe wave before setting out across the field toward the tower. The vegetation was thready on the baked soil, and dust rose around her ankles despite her light tread. There was a faint herbal scent to the sun-filled air, and the stones of the Moorish tower looming up ahead were bleached by the strong light. Old age had played havoc with the limestone blocks on the top, leaving them uneven and worn where the weather had taken its toll. The bottom of the structure was in better shape, although the single archway leading to the interior was stained and discolored. Undoubtedly the herd of goats had more than a nodding acquaintance with the old ruin, Jennifer decided as she approached.

There were other evidences of habitation, as well. A scattered row of mud nests occupied a small ledge ten feet above the ground, and as Jennifer paused to stare up at them, she heard a persistent buzzing and wondered if a beehive was on the top of the tower as well.

A soft tinkling noise from the bellwether goat brought her attention back to ground level, and she smiled as she watched the herd continue to move toward her as they grazed. They were a mottled group; some white and some bearing patches of brown but all liberally coated with the dust which rose around them as they foraged in the sparse grass. Jennifer looked idly for their herder but without success; probably he was still napping up by the road in the shade. Then she glanced back to the car where she could see Reed in the front seat, intent on his film changing. Her lips curved in a smile as she surveyed him. Later, she'd suggest buying picture postcards and see what reaction she'd get.

She turned back to the tower and walked around to the far side, giving the arch plenty of leeway. If Reed wanted to investigate that shadowy interior, he was more than welcome to do it—alone. The sudden flight of a bird overhead made her wonder if there might even be bats in the murky darkness. She shivered and then laughed at herself. Elias certainly had emerged unscathed.

Nonetheless, she kept a prudent distance until she rounded the corner and found herself on the cliff edge, with an unspoiled view of the Mediterranean before her.

Clouds looked like puffballs in the pale blue sky and the deeper, jewel-like tones of the water made her content to stand and stare in wonder. There was the outline of a freighter headed toward the Libyan coast, the wake still discernible as the propeller rode high in the water. Still farther away, smoke from the funnel of a cruise ship etched a smudged line on the horizon.

Then, suddenly, the tranquillity of the afternoon was shattered by a rising crescendo of noise; a demoniac shriek that made Jennifer jump and sent her adrenalin soaring when she saw how close she'd ventured to the cliff edge. But even as she turned back toward safety, she became aware that she wasn't the only one scared out of her wits by the yelling; the goats had panicked as well. Their instinctive reaction was to get as far away from the noise as possible. Some of the flock scattered toward the hill, but most of the two dozen animals obeyed another instinct—to follow the bellwether leader. She was a big brown-and-white creature who pounded down the hillside toward the tower and then at the last minute swerved away from the archway to stay out in the open. The thudding of hoofs on the sun-baked earth warned Jennifer of the herd's coming even before the swirling melange of terrified, bleating animals surged around the corner and were upon her.

She fought frantically to maintain her balance in their midst—to withstand their plunge toward the cliffside even before the animals themselves scented the new danger and milled in a half circle to escape it.

For an instant she thought she saw the herder coming to her rescue. Then pain streaked through her leg and her eyes filled with tears as a panicky animal trampled her shin. When she was able to see again, the robed figure had disappeared.

By then, she was struggling even to breathe in the crush of the stampeding herd. She could only gulp at the dust-laden air with the stinking smell of death upon it. Survival consisted of battling to stay upright—trying to move toward the tower even if the gain was in inches—rather than be shoved over the sheer cliff face.

Desperation gave her added strength, but even that wasn't enough, and she was finally dragged down to the ground. Her last remembrance was trying to protect her head from the goats' sharp hooves and then, with awful finality, the bitter taste of dust in her mouth.

Chapter Three

Jennifer had no real knowledge of what happened after that.

She could only recall that one moment there was merciful blackness; the next, she was propped in a sitting position, listening to a graphic and remarkably profane description of goats in general and Maltese goats in particular. She waited until the end of the diatribe before lifting her head from Reed's chest and saying, "They *are* gone, aren't they?" Despite her efforts, her voice wobbled treacherously.

"They're gone," he confirmed, sounding as if he'd like to start swearing all over again. "Everybody's gone—including the damn fool idiot who was supposed to be watching over them. I hope he has to chase them into the next county to round them up." Reed put her gently at arm's length and kept his tone casual. "Before I carry you to the car, I'd better check out some facts. Any trouble taking a deep breath—pain when you move—that sort of thing?"

Jennifer experimented and then shook her head in relief. "Nothing serious—just the grandmother of all headaches. Oh!" Her voice went up in alarm as her fingers found a bloody bruise at her hairline.

"You lost a little skin," Reed put in hurriedly. "On your shin, too."

"That's not bad." For the first time, she let her gaze search the now-deserted hillside. The remnants of the goat herd were barely visible up by the road, browsing on sparse tufts of grass as they wandered along. "They look so normal now," she said, her voice sounding thin and frightened. "My god, what happened to them? A few minutes ago they almost got me killed. What made that terrible noise and sent them off? And why didn't the herder try to help? When I saw him come out of the tower, he ran the other way."

Reed lifted her gently to her feet and then swung her up in his arms. "We'll talk about it later in the car," was all he said. And when she would have protested, he added, "Be quiet! You can play the independent woman another time."

Jennifer wanted to say that independent womanhood had nothing to do with it—she was perfectly capable of walking. Then she realized that she wasn't; the only way she could have gotten to the car by herself was on all fours, and she infinitely preferred the comfort of his arms. She let her eyelids droop to keep out that blazing sun and only raised them again when they reached the car. "I hope I wasn't too heavy," she murmured, because she didn't know what else to say.

His grin was lopsided. "I'll survive, but if you're going to make a habit of this, you'll have to skip desserts." As he spoke, he was opening the car door and assisting her onto the seat. "You say that you saw the herder coming out of the tower in the midst of the confusion?"

"I'm sure I did. Didn't you?" She stared down at the old ruin to check. "But you can't see the archway from here, can you?"

"Not from this angle. All I could hear was that hellish commotion." He hesitated for an instant and added levelly, "I remember seeing the herder headed toward the village before the fracas started."

"But if he went that way, then who did *I* see?"

"Damned if I know. Do you feel up to waiting an extra five minutes while I search that tower?"

"Yes, of course—but maybe there's still someone there."

He reached in and touched her shoulder to reassure her. "Relax, honey! Our only bird has flown. My guess is that he wanted some confusion so he could escape in the middle of it." Reed straightened and started down toward the tower. "Lean on the horn if you need me."

Jennifer watched until he disappeared around the corner of the old ruin and then checked the road behind her. By that time the last goat had vanished and silence had settled once more on the warm hillside. Valletta might have been a million miles away instead of just at the other end of the island. Jennifer drew an uneasy breath, realizing that the isolation which had been so attractive before now held a foreboding quiality.

As she sat back, she caught a glimpse of herself in the side mirror and gave a moan of despair. It was a wonder Reed hadn't fled in the opposite direction when he'd picked her up off the ground. Blood was mixed with dust at her forehead and the resultant red mud streaks gave her a bizarre, clownlike appearance. This, coupled with her gray complexion and distinctly grimy chin, made her a surefire winner for "Hallowe'en Haunt of the Year."

She started to scrub off some of the dirt with her handkerchief, keeping a weather eye on the tower for Reed's reappearance. When she finally saw his tall figure come around the corner of the tower, she gave a conscious sigh of relief.

He didn't waste any time getting back to the car, but there was a frown on his face that made Jennifer ask, "What's wrong?" as soon as he came within hearing distance.

He didn't answer until he got in and closed the door. Then he opened his hand to display a torn and stained piece of cloth on his palm. "Does this mean anything to you?" he asked, watching her closely.

She started to touch the scrap and then drew

her fingers back fastidiously. "Those dark streaks," she said faintly. "Are they blood?"

Reed nodded.

She bent again to examine it before she looked up, stricken. "Elias was wearing a shirt in this shade of lavender. The style was pretty far out—that's why I remember. My god, you didn't find any . . . any . . ."

"Bruised and battered bodies? Not a one. Nor any packages, either. Probably Elias just caught his sleeve on a nail when he was making the delivery," Reed went on glibly, wanting to kick himself for having exhibited the piece of cloth in the first place. The terrified expression on Jennifer's face showed that this new development had put her on the edge of hysteria. He reached over to shove the material out of sight in the glove compartment and hastily started the car. "It's time I got you to a doctor," he said, reversing and turning to reach the main road.

His soothing tone made Jennifer's temper flare. "Don't treat me like an idiot," she snapped, opening the glove compartment and taking out the piece of material again. "There was nothing wrong with Elias's shirt when he drove me to the hotel. I'm almost positive."

Her reaction was a relief to the man beside her. Anger was far better therapy for shock than withdrawal. It would also help to keep her mind off her injuries until he could get her to a hospital. "I doubt if you inspected his shirt tail when he got back in the car," Reed drawled, applying his foot heavily to the accelerator once they reached the hard-surfaced road and turned back toward Valletta.

"You're wrong there." Her voice was flat but emphatic as she put the cloth away again. "It was the kind of sport shirt you wear outside, and short-sleeved, as well. I know for a fact that it wasn't torn and I didn't see any blood when Elias came back to the car." She half-turned in the seat, wincing as she moved. "You didn't find anything else in the tower?"

Reed decided to be honest. "There were more bloodstains on the dirt inside, but it could be animal blood. Hell! Maybe they use that place for slaughtering their herd. We're going to feel like a couple of numbskulls when we get back and find Elias sitting in the hotel parking lot."

"You could be right," she said slowly. "I suppose that man I saw in the tower was frightened when he discovered what he'd done and ..."

". . . decided to run rather than hang around and get the blame," Reed finished for her. "Was he close enough to recognize?"

"Oh, no." She slid down and rested her head against the back of the seat, hoping to make the throbbing subside. "All I could see was the back of a robed figure running away. He had a funny bobbing motion—sort of a dot and carry."

"It doesn't matter. We had no more business

around the place than he did. If he'd stopped to think, he needn't have lit out the way he did." Reed slowed to turn onto a more heavily traveled highway, leading to the capital. "I'm sorry that you had such a rotten experience. So much for picnic lunches."

"I was having a great time until then."

"So was I." He shot an anxious look toward her quiet figure. "You can go straight to bed once we get back to the hotel. If the doctor doesn't have other ideas."

Jennifer turned to frown at him. "What kind of ideas?" she asked sharply.

Her abruptness caught him offguard. "Well . . . I don't know. Who can tell what doctors will dream up? He might want to keep you in the hospital overnight as a precaution."

"Oh, no! I'm not going. You either take me back to the hotel or the airport."

"Now look here—"

Jennifer turned away and ignored his attempt to get a word in. "You're not parking me in a Maltese hospital where I don't know a soul while you go zipping off to Egypt. I'll take a plane home first."

If she'd been looking anywhere but straight ahead, she would have seen Reed's eyes narrow to ominous slits. "You're not taking a plane anywhere," he announced just as definitely. "The way you look now, they'd show you the door if you even tried to buy a ticket. We're going to the hospital here if I have to drag you in kicking and screaming. Chances are, the doctors will just bandage your bruised shin and prescribe pills for your headache, but it's a damn shame they can't do something to corral that temper of yours while they're about it."

"Anything else?" she asked icily after an unfriendly pause.

"I think that covers it."

"So do I." She shot his profile a furious look. "I take back what I said about your zipping off to Egypt. You can leave anytime as far as I'm concerned."

Her tirade didn't even dent his assurance. "Wouldn't think of it," he said, sounding amused rather than angry. "After all, I promised Jeremy." As she opened her mouth to tell him what she thought about that, he shook his head and got in first. "Remember, he's still depending on you for that thesis of his. You'd better simmer down now or you'll sizzle the mercury when they take your temperature. And I can reassure you on one other thing—you won't be thrown away in Malta no matter what the doctor says. You're my responsibility until this project is over."

"Thanks very much," Jennifer responded tiredly, wishing she could tell him to go to hell. There wasn't a woman alive who would want to be tabbed as a responsibility by an eligible man.

"You're awfully quiet." There was a shade of anxiety in Reed's tone when he finally spoke again. "You're not feeling worse, are you? We're almost on the outskirts of Valletta now, but I can't risk driving any faster in this damned traffic. The hospital's just over the next hill."

"I'm all right," she assured him. Honesty made her add, "Really, I'm feeling better. Now I just have an occasional urge to hit you over the head with something heavy."

"Great," he said drily. "It doesn't sound like there's a chance of getting rid of you overnight."

A little later when he was turning into the curving drive of a large brick hospital, her fears came back. "Will you come with me?" she asked in a small voice.

"All the way—unless they throw me out of the emergency room or whatever. Even then, I'll wait in the hall." He turned off the motor and gave her a reassuring smile. "Don't worry, honey. This shouldn't take long, and you'll feel better once you get your face washed."

She *did* feel better when he ushered her into a modern emergency room with stainless-steel equipment and helpful nurses in starched white uniforms. The young doctor who examined her was kind and tactful, as well, speaking English with a distinct British accent. He frowned when he checked the abrasion on her head and gave strict orders about bandaging her leg. Her bounding pulse rate also concerned him, but he didn't reveal it; instead, he simply asked Reed to accompany him to the dispensary for some medication to take with them. "She's still suffering from shock," he announced once they were out of Jennifer's hearing. "I'd suggest we keep her overnight only I think she'd recover faster in familiar surroundings. Is there someone who can care for her at the hotel tonight?"

"I'll be there . . . if that'll do."

The doctor nodded in agreement. "She doesn't need intensive nursing—just someone to look in now and then. The sedative I'm giving should provide the rest she needs, but I don't want her upset in any way."

"You don't have to worry. Shall I bring her back in the morning?"

"It would be best." The doctor wrote the dosage on a packet of tablets and handed them to Reed. "She's lucky to be traveling with a friend at a time like this."

"Miss Rogers is just working for me," Reed told him, intent on setting the record straight.

The doctor was undaunted by his reproof. "Then I won't have to prescribe a sedative for you during this night nursing stint." He was grinning broadly as he led the way back to the emergency room. "No wonder you American businessmen forge ahead—you don't allow yourselves any attractive diversions."

"I wouldn't go so far as to say that," Reed hedged.

"Then you won't mind bringing Miss Rogers back for her checkup tomorrow."

"Not at all." Reed responded with a grin of his own. "Who knows? By then, I might need those tranquilizers, after all."

He was careful to keep such thoughts from Jennifer, however, when he shepherded her out of the hospital emergency exit and installed her carefully back in the car. She must have closed her eyes after that because it seemed only an instant later before the car stopped again. Lifting her eyelids took longer than usual and when she finally succeeded, Reed was already opening her door.

"Thought I'd park here in the shade," he said, helping her to get out. "There's a side door to the hotel just down the walk, so you won't have to go through the lobby. I'd hate to have people think that I'd been beating you," he added lightly.

By that time, Jennifer felt so fuzzy that she would have taken a swan dive into the shallow end of the pool if he'd suggested it. She simply nodded and let him guide her along the path into the air-conditioned comfort of their hotel.

There was an elevator just inside the door and, as they pushed the call button and waited, Jennifer observed that Reed was staring intently back into the parking lot through the glass door they'd entered. She put it to the back of her mind, however, because the elevator arrived just then and whisked them to the upper floor. The hotel corridor was deserted, too, and Reed matched his steps to Jennifer's slower pace, keeping a grip on her arm for support. He saw her start to fumble through her purse and calmly reached down to take it from her when they got to her room. Without comment he extracted the key, unlocked the door, and ushered her in.

"I don't need any more help," she informed him when she stood in the middle of the room. "I can manage from here on by myself." Unfortunately, she backed into the edge of the mattress as she said it and sat down unceremoniously.

Reed shook his head. "You'll never convince me of that. Tell you what—I'll go and get Louise to help you. She's a little on the fruitcake side, but underneath she's okay. I'll be back after she's gotten you undressed."

"Reed, please—I don't want to make explanations now."

"You won't have to say anything," he told her. "I'll cook up a story."

"By tomorrow, you'll have thought of a better one. Honestly, if you really want to help me—go and order some tea. I'll be in bed by the time it comes."

"Okay, but if you're not, I'll take things into my own hands when I get back." He paused halfway through the hall door. "And, for pete's sake, don't pass out in the bathroom over the tiled floor."

"I'll make sure I'm over the rug," she assured him solemnly.

Getting into a pair of pajamas took considerable will power on her part; only Reed's threat kept her going when she was tempted to kick off her shoes and simply crawl under the covers as she was. But when she'd donned a pair of cool nylon pajamas, she was glad that she'd made the effort. After that there was barely time for her to get into bed before she heard a brief rap on the door.

Reed came in without any more formalities. His glance raked over her. "I wanted to make sure you were receiving," he said, and disappeared back into the hall. An instant later he returned, this time followed by a waiter carrying a tea tray. The man deposited it on the bureau and left without a word's being spoken.

When they were alone again, Reed issued a new set of orders, "One pill, one cup of tea, and then it's bedtime for you. The doctor said to make sure you were horizontal before you took the medicine."

Jennifer watched him pour some water from the insulated carafe on the bedside table and hand her a glass before he reached in his shirt pocket for a small packet.

"What's in this?" she wanted to know when he handed her one of the pills from it.

"Who knows? Maltese doctors aren't any more talkative than American ones." Reed went over to pour her some tea and brought the cup back to the bed. "He wants you to get some rest before he sees you tomorrow. After that, I'll chain you to the typewriter."

A little color crept into her cheeks at his teasing, and she swallowed the pill meekly.

Reed leaned against the edge of the bureau as he drank his tea. His attention was ostensibly on a tourist magazine, but he was also keeping a close watch on Jennifer as she rested against the pillow, holding her cup in both hands. "Want me to take that for you?" he asked finally.

"All right, thanks." She stared at him owlishly. "I'm beginning to see two of you. Either that pill is starting to work or I'm drunk."

"On just one cup of tea," he said lightly as he put it back on the tray. "That's what I'd call a cheap date."

Jennifer put out a hand to detain him when he came back to the bedside. "I've just remembered what I meant to ask you. Was Elias in the parking lot when we came back?" When Reed didn't answer, she tried to sit up straighter and hang on to the sheet which was covering her at the same time. "Reed, you did look for him, didn't you?"

He reached down and calmly tucked the sheet around her again. "Yes, I looked. I didn't see him when we came back, so after I'd ordered the tea, I went out to ask some of the other drivers and the doorman. None of them had seen Elias since he dropped you off this forenoon."

"Then it must have been a piece of his shirt you found in the tower. Something's happened to him—I'm sure of it. The way it almost happened to me." She bit her lip and then looked beseechingly up at his tall figure. "Reed, you won't be far away, will you? Until this darned pill wears off?"

He bent down then and gently made her lie back against the pillow. He kept his hands on her shoulders, pushing aside the thin pajama top so he could smooth her tense muscles. "Don't worry, honey, I'll be around," was all he said, but it was enough to make her smile before her lashes fluttered wearily down.

Chapter Four

The sleeping pill was so effective that Jennifer remembered absolutely nothing for some hours. After that, the effect of the drug lessened and she started to relive those painful earlier happenings. This made her come completely awake in the middle of the night, with her heart pounding as she struggled to sit up.

Then she discovered Reed sitting on the edge of the bed beside her. "Take it easy—you've just had a bad dream," he was saying when she finally recognized him in the dim light from a lamp on the dressing table.

She looked around dazedly and saw a rumpled blanket tossed over the upholstered chair by the balcony. "Have you been here all this time?"

"The doctor thought I'd better keep an eye on you." He pushed off the mattress and stood up, stretching. "Sometimes sedatives affect people in different ways."

"I was having a terrible dream," she murmured, hoping she didn't look as bad as she suspected.

If she did, Reed gave no indication. He just

said, "Now that you're awake, you'd better take another pill."

"No, please . . . I don't need one. I'm sleepy enough." The armchair and blanket drew her gaze back like a magnet. "You must have been terribly uncomfortable," she said flatly. "And it's awful sleeping with your clothes on."

"I'll survive," he told her. "Sure you don't want another pill?" When she shook her head, he went over to turn off the lamp. "Better get back to sleep then," he suggested before going back to his chair.

The faint gleam of moonlight that seeped through the curtains showed him pulling the blanket around him. Jennifer watched for a minute or two and then felt compelled to say, "If you want to go back to your room now, I'll be fine. Honestly, you don't have to worry about me any more."

"If you don't belt up and go back to sleep," he cut in levelly, "you'll get another pill whether you want it or not. Good night, Jennifer."

Since his presence in the room provided a comforting warmth, she surrendered and snuggled down into her pillow. Perhaps later there'd be some way she could repay him. It was on that highly unoriginal thought that her eyelids came down . . . this time to stay.

When she opened them the next time it was broad daylight. She noticed sunshine streaming through the balcony curtains and, at the same time, felt the mattress under her move slightly. For a panicky second, she was sure Malta was undergoing an earthquake tremor. Then she heard a partially stifled groan and she rolled over to glimpse Reed's broad back as he sat on the edge of the bed. The way the blanket was tossed back showed that it had been covering both of them for the last part of the night. Reed was still fully dressed, she noted thankfully, but he looked like a man who ached in every bone. She wriggled nervously and cleared her throat.

The noise made Reed shift abruptly on the mattress to look at her. "You're awake," he said at last. The inane comment showed that he wasn't finding it easy to start a conversation either. He went on awkwardly, "I'm sorry. I didn't mean to wake you up. That damned chair"—he jerked his head toward the offending piece of furniture—"felt like it was made out of cast iron. I hope you don't mind my trading it for the other side of your mattress."

"Of course not," Jennifer said, trying to sound as if it was a common occurrence. In the harsh morning light, the lines on his face looked deeper than usual, and if his studied movements were any indication, he had a monumental headache as well. "Did you get any sleep?" she asked finally.

"Enough." Reed stood up and rubbed his

thumb along his jaw, grimacing as he felt the bristle.

Jennifer could sympathize with his discomfort, wishing she knew how to get a robe from her suitcase on the other side of the room without making a mad dash for it.

Her distress must have gotten through to Reed even in his weary state. His eyes gleamed with suppressed laughter as he walked across and plucked her travel robe from an opened suitcase. "I imagine you could use this. You can have first turn in the bathroom while I order coffee." He dropped the robe on the bed and reached for the telephone to call room service.

When she saw him calmly turn his back, Jennifer felt like an idiot for worrying about sheer pajamas. She shrugged into her robe and stood up beside the bed to belt it. Another glance at Reed's preoccupied figure gave her an annoyed twinge—he didn't have to be so blatant in his lack of interest. Then she saw her reflection in the mirror across the room and didn't linger any longer.

She made all the repairs possible in the bathroom and hoped that neatly combed hair and makeup would help to hide the translucent quality of her complexion and the weary smudges under her eyes.

Reed was kind enough not to comment on them when she finally emerged. Somehow in the interval he'd managed to shave and comb his hair. "I made a quick detour down the hall to my room," he explained, taking her key out of his pocket and dropping it back on the dressing table. " 'Fraid I had to lock you in while I was gone."

"That's all right. I'm sure none of these precautions are necessary," she said apologetically. "It was silly of me to cause such a fuss just because Elias took an afternoon off. I'll bet that he's back at work today."

"You're probably right. There's no reason not to use him for a little sightseeing here in Valletta after you check with the doctor. That is, if you feel up to it."

"I feel fine," Jennifer said, knowing that she wasn't going to miss anything just because she creaked in a few places.

Reed was watching her closely. "It's a good thing you're not under oath, but coffee should help. The only thing that sounds better right now is going back to bed . . ."

A knock on the door interrupted him.

"You'd better answer it," Jennifer said. "You have more clothes on."

"Room-service waiters are used to anything," Reed commented, but he waited until she had stepped back into the bathroom before he opened the hall door. "Come in, you made good time," he said, his voice trailing off when he recognized the figure on the threshold. "Louise, what in the devil are you doing here?"

"I could ask the same thing of you, Reed darling." The secretary was dressed for the day in a white ruffled blouse and a well-fitting green gabardine skirt. There wasn't a hair out of place in her bouffant coiffure, and her makeup was impeccable. "This *is* Jennifer's room, isn't it?"

"Yes, of course." He stepped back and motioned her in.

Her glance went over his mussed slacks and wrinkled shirt like a rapier. "Good heavens, what in the world have you been doing?" she exclaimed and then discovered Jennifer's robed figure standing hesitantly in the bathroom doorway. "I'm so sorry—I had no idea that I was interrupting anything."

"Oh, for god's sake, Louise, stop acting like the local censorship board," Reed growled. "Jennifer was involved in an accident yesterday and I've just been making sure that she took her pills. It was either that or the doctor would have kept her in the hospital."

"And I didn't want to stay there," Jennifer put in, deciding it was time for reinforcements. Louise was the last person she wanted to see just then, but she couldn't let her think that Reed was to blame in any way. "Dr. Whitney has been very kind."

"I'm sure he has." The other's tone couldn't be faulted, but she didn't miss the rumpled bed with its two dented pillows at the head. "You should have called me. I would have been glad to help."

"I was going to wait and see how I felt after

some coffee. Dr. Whitney ordered it a little while ago."

"You might as well call him Reed," Louise said, settling in the much-maligned upholstered chair. "It seems silly to be formal when we'll all be working and traveling together."

"Reed . . . then." Jennifer kept her glance away from her employer, whom she knew was thoroughly enjoying the ridiculous exchange.

Fortunately, there was another knock at the door just then and he went over to admit the room-service waiter and his cart. "I'll have him bring another cup for you, Louise."

"It isn't necessary. Edwin and I just finished breakfast in the coffee shop. You two go ahead—don't bother getting dressed on my account." She ignored the silence that followed her bright comment and waited until the waiter had closed the door before she extracted a newspaper from her big shoulder bag. "As a matter of fact, it was Edwin who thought you should see this article on the front page. I went to your room first, Reed, but when I didn't get any answer there, I thought I might just take a chance and check with Jennifer. Most young secretaries know the whereabouts of their employers." Her archness made Jennifer turn scarlet and tempted Reed to upend the coffee pot over Louise's suspiciously golden head.

"You must have just missed me," he said finally. "What's so important in the paper?"

Louise handed him her copy of the *Times* of

Malta. "Probably it's nothing—at least, that's what Franz thinks. But you know Edwin."

Reed glanced at her over the top of the page, barely controlling his impatience. "Since I don't have the faintest idea of what you're talking about, it's hard to have an opinion."

Louise's thin eyebrows went up. "Really, Reed, you *are* in a temper this morning. It's that article at the bottom of the page about the man injured on the cliffs."

Louise was concentrating on Reed so she didn't see Jennifer's sudden look of alarm or the way the younger woman sagged against the frame of the bathroom door. "What man?" Jennifer asked huskily as Reed folded the paper back.

"Elias somebody or other," Louise informed her. "Edwin wondered if he could possibly be the man Reed hired the other day. The article says something about the victim being a taxidriver." She turned back to Whitney. "Why don't you read it aloud? That way it saves time."

There wasn't any way of avoiding her request. Reed kept his attention focused on the newspaper as he read,

A man in his late twenties, tentatively identified as Elias Ferrugia, was injured critically yesterday on the sheer cliffs near Benghaisa Point. Mr. Ferrugia, who is a taxidriver from Rabat, is believed to have fallen sometime during the afternoon and was discovered unconscious by fishermen in the early evening. Authorities are searching for his next of kin to establish positive identification. Doctors at St. Luke's Hospital, Gwardamanga, do not hold much hope for the victim's recovery.

When Reed finished reading, there was a perceptible pause. Then Louise said, "Well, what do you think? I told Edwin and Franz that you'd know if anyone would."

Reed took his time about folding up the paper and handing it back to her. "Sorry to disappoint you," he said finally. "I didn't pay any attention to Elias's last name when I hired him."

"Do you remember if he mentioned being from Rabat?"

Reed rubbed the back of his hand over his forehead. "Lord, no. Who discusses home towns when you're hiring a temporary driver? Why don't you call the hospital?"

"Edwin already did," she reported smugly. "The doctors say they've postponed trying for positive identification because of the man's condition. Apparently the physical damage was ... extensive."

Jennifer shuddered at Louise's tactful phrasing. It was small wonder the man remained nameless considering the height of the cliff she'd seen yesterday. Her glance was perturbed as she got Reed's attention. "Where is Benghaisa Point?"

Louise interrupted, "I doubt if you've heard of it. It's way down at the south end of the island. Edwin and Franz drove me past it the first day we were here. I remember because the name was the same as the place in Libya. This one overlooks a place called Pretty Bay . . . why, what's the matter?" Her voice rose in distress as Jennifer swayed on her feet. "Oh, my dear, you should be lying down. I don't know why Reed let you get up in the first place." She was over assisting Jennifer solicitously before Reed could move from the other side of the room. Whatever suspicions she'd entertained in the beginning were abruptly discarded; just then Jennifer needed nursing by someone other than a mere man. "What did the doctor say?" Louise asked Reed, a new note of authority in her voice.

"Practically nothing," he replied. "She has to go back for a checkup this morning."

"I wish you wouldn't talk about me as if I weren't here," Jennifer complained. "And there's certainly no reason for you to change your plans for the day. I'll be fine, really."

"Perhaps." Louise wasn't about to let a genuine invalid slip through her fingers without exploring all possibilities. She gave Jennifer a consoling pat. "You have your coffee, dear, while I hurry down to tell Edwin and Franz where I am. Then I'll come back and help you get dressed for the doctor."

"Really, there's no need." Jennifer protested.

Louise cut in, "I wouldn't think of anything else. Reed can go and get changed as well. Sometimes I think he forgets that he's not still in the middle of the jungle."

"Now *I've* become invisible," her target complained to Jennifer. "I didn't know that a wrinkled shirt had such an effect on women."

"It does as far as I'm concerned." Louise got up and headed for the door. "Remember to pour some coffee for Jennifer before you go."

Louise had barely closed the door behind her when Jennifer shot a worried glance at Reed and said, "That accident report in the newspaper happened near Pretty Bay and that's where we were yesterday. It must be Elias in the hospital. Reed—you'll have to go find out."

"Take it easy, honey, I will." He poured the coffee and brought a cup to her but kept hold of it when he saw how her fingers trembled. "Here, take a swallow," he instructed, before going back to the other topic. "I'll do what I can, but it sounds as if the man's in intensive care. That means no visitors will be allowed at this point. Probably the authorities have his personal effects, though. They might want me to check those for identification."

"And if you find it is our Elias—what then?"

He handed over the coffee cup and rubbed

At 6 for 99¢, you can afford 6 new fantasies this month.

Get more romance in The Doubleday Book Club.

Here's how our club plan works.

You'll get your 6 books for only 99¢ plus shipping and handling along with your FREE Tote Bag when accepted as a member. If not satisfied, return them within 10 days to cancel your membership and owe nothing.

About every 4 weeks (14 times a year) you'll receive our magazine describing our two Club Selections and at least 100 Alternates. *The Extra-Value Selection is always just $2.98 (up to 60% off publishers' edition prices.)* The Featured Selection and Alternates save you an average of 50% off publishers' edition prices. A charge is added for shipping and handling.

If you want both Club Selections, do nothing — they will be shipped automatically. If you'd prefer only one

Selection, an Alternate or no book at all, indicate this on the order form and return it before the date specified. You'll have at least 10 days. If you do *not* have 10 days and receive books you don't want, return them at our expense.

Once you've purchased just 6 books during your first year of membership, you may resign or continue with no further purchase obligation.

The Doubleday Book Club offers its own complete hard-bound editions, sometimes altered in size to fit special presses and save members even more.

The Doubleday Book Club
Makes your fantasies affordable.

STAR WARS
GEORGE LUCAS
2089

Helen
Van Slyke
*Always
is not
Forever*
The New York Times
2188

RUNNING
FOR HEALTH AND BEAUTY
A Complete Guide for Women
Kathryn Lance
2592

The
SESAME STREET
ABC
STORYBOOK
6452

The
FAN
7716

ROBIN COOK
2162

The Encyclopedia of
HINTS & DOLLAR STRETCHERS
2576

Fun
STORYBOOK
Ever

his chin thoughtfully. "Then I suppose I tell them all I know."

"Will I have to make a statement?"

"Not if I can help it. Damn it all—this is just what I was trying to avoid. I'd hoped to put you on that car ferry and forget all about yesterday afternoon."

She took a deep breath and surveyed him squarely, "Elias didn't have that chance."

"We don't *know* that he's the one involved."

Jennifer made a tired grimace. "You don't have to be tactful. Incidentally, you'd better get out of here before Louise comes back. She's probably already passed on the news about your spending the night here."

Reed muttered something profane and then said, "I'd have stayed in that damned chair if I hadn't weakened about four A.M." His expression was sheepish. "I meant to lie down on the bed just long enough to get the kinks out, but then I fell sound asleep."

"You don't have to explain," Jennifer protested, "I understand perfectly."

"That will make two of us against the multitude. You're right about Louise—she's not one to let any juicy tidbits stay unpublicized. Ed and Franz will get a blow-by-blow account."

"I don't mind if you don't," Jennifer replied smiling. "Once they get a look at my bruises, they'll really wonder what happened."

"I'm glad you can see the amusing side," he said, grinning himself. "Now I'd better go and change clothes. I'll come back to pick you up in half an hour. Then we'll have breakfast and take a cab to the hospital. Okay?"

Jennifer shook her head slowly. "I'd rather you wouldn't wait to see the police. It's easy for me to get to the hospital on my own. Once I'm through with the doctor, I can meet you wherever you say."

Louise stuck her head back around the door in time to hear the last sentence. "My dear, you don't have to worry about a thing. I've told Edwin that I'll be busy all morning taking care of you." She eyed Reed disparagingly. "I thought you'd gone."

"I'm on my way." He turned back to Jennifer. "Want to meet me in town when you're finished?"

"We're going to join Edwin and Franz by the cathedral before lunch," Louise told him firmly. "You can come along if you like. Jennifer might enjoy some sightseeing before we leave Malta." Her head swung around to the younger woman. "Men never think of things like that. We can go shopping, too—if the doctor allows it."

"I'm beginning to understand why Ed is so well organized," Reed said somewhat bitterly as he walked over to the door. "At the main entrance to the cathedral then, around a quarter to twelve."

Louise shooed him out and turned back to her patient. "There, now—I'll start the water for your shower. A bath would be too hard to manage if you have to keep that bandage on your leg dry. Then I'll order a proper breakfast for you here in the room. It's so much less trouble than going downstairs."

Her plans made such sense that Jennifer capitulated without arguing. When she emerged from the shower a little later and came back into the bedroom, she felt obligated to say, "It's nice of you to take such trouble. I hope that this isn't spoiling any plans of yours."

"Not a thing." The other woman had the coffee tray ready for removal when the waiter came just then with the breakfast order. She signed the check and sent him on his way before seating herself across the table from Jennifer. "Edwin has been in Malta before, so I have a terrible time getting him to stir away from the hotel once he's finished work. The dining room and the swimming pool are usually the only things he's interested in." Her thin lips curved in a triumphant smile. "When I told him that this afternoon was your only chance to see Valletta, both he and Franz agreed to accompany us—without arguing, either."

Jennifer wasn't thrilled by the prospect of a long, group sightseeing tour and wondered what Reed's reaction would be when he heard about it.

"I think it's important to be taken around by experts," Louise went on, ignoring any undercurrents. "Actually, Franz offered to take you on his own because he's spent so much time photographing the places of interest here, but I told him that we all needed to get to know each other. This is a much better chance than the ship."

"Oh, why's that?"

"I get queasy the minute we leave the harbor," Louise confessed. "Even if there isn't a wave in sight. Silly, isn't it?"

The older woman didn't need any encouragement to continue monopolizing the conversation. She scarcely waited for Jennifer to start on scrambled eggs and toast before she was telling about her job as secretary to Edwin Rudolph. "Such a demanding man in his work," she confided in the tone of a woman well able to cope with such stress. "And since he's a bachelor, he has no personal distractions. Probably that's why he's done so well in his career with the Foundation. He's absolutely tops dealing with water resources."

"I see," Jennifer said, feeling a response was needed.

"Since I'm in the same situation, we make a good combination," Louise went on, brushing a crumb from the tablecloth.

"You mean you specialize in water-power projects, too?"

"Heavens, no." Louise gave an exasperated trill of laughter. "I mean that I'm not married, either. Not now," she added. "You understand?"

Jennifer almost said, "Not really," but smiled instead and changed the subject. "Is Franz involved in water power, as well?"

Louise waved a deprecating hand. "Oh, he's just Edwin's assistant and does the driving or odd jobs. I will say that he's good at languages. That's not surprising, because he's from Munich and Europeans *have* to be multilingual."

"I wish I'd met more Europeans like him," Jennifer said ruefully. "The Frenchmen I met spoke only French, and the Portuguese spoke only Portuguese."

Louise's eyes narrowed. "What were you doing in Portugal? I didn't think the Foundation was working there."

"It was Madeira and I was meeting Reed . . . I mean, Dr. Whitney. My brother wanted me to give him a message." Jennifer was aware how lame her excuse sounded as she related it.

Even if she hadn't been, Louise's expression would have shown her. "Oh, Reed . . . the things that man gets away with!" The other woman shook her head reprovingly. "I hope your brother warned you not to take him seriously. A woman friend of mine at the Foundation wasn't so lucky. You understand?"

Evidently those last two words were a favorite expression for Louise. This time, Jennifer wasn't so diplomatic. "No," she said flatly. "I *don't* understand. What happened?"

"From what I hear, he led the poor woman

on dreadfully. Then he was assigned to that project in Africa and simply walked off and left her."

Jennifer made a grimace of distaste. "There are stories like that going around no matter what job you have."

Louise drew back, affronted. "That may be, but I still think your Dr. Whitney plays fast and loose with anything in skirts."

A telling silence followed, and finally Jennifer pushed her plate away. Scrambled eggs suddenly had no appeal, and for the first time in an hour, she became conscious of a nagging headache.

"My dear, you should try and eat more," Louise pressed solicitously. "You won't feel like doing any sightseeing later on without a decent breakfast."

"No, thanks, I can't manage another thing. I'll make up for it at lunch." Jennifer looked at her watch and stood up. "If we're going to stay on schedule, I'd better check with the doctor."

"I'll be right with you," Louise said, pushing back her own chair. "There shouldn't be any trouble getting a taxi at this time. I wonder if that Elias in the newspaper account is the same one Reed hired," she went on while checking her lipstick at the dressing table. "He seemed nice enough, didn't you think?" Her bland gaze met Jennifer's in the mirror. "You must have been one of the last people to see him alive. Oh, dear, now what have I said—you look dreadfully pale."

Her chirping commentary made Jennifer want to pick up the nearest lamp and heave it at the other's carefully coiffed wig. Louise must have used different tactics with Edwin, she decided, or he would have done the same thing months ago. Until that moment, the man hadn't aroused any feelings in Jennifer, but just then she gave him full marks for restraint. "No wonder he's a confirmed bachelor," she murmured out loud.

Louise thankfully misunderstood. "Reed? Who knows what's on his mind. Other than the usual thing," she added darkly. "You understand?"

"I'll get a hat and be right with you," Jennifer said with some determination. "I think this Malta sun has already gone to my head."

"There are some marvelous shops in Valletta," Louise confided to Jennifer when they were in a taxi headed toward the center of the city. "I've been buying Maltese crosses ever since I arrived." She bent forward to show the one she was wearing around her neck on a silver chain. "This is inlaid with amethyst, but they sell them in all sorts of materials. They told me each point of the cross represents one of the Beatitudes from the Sermon on the Mount."

"I didn't know that," Jennifer was examining

it with interest. "I thought the Maltese cross was a result of the Knights settling here."

"Edwin will love you. He's been spending all of his spare time reading about the trouble the Knights of St. John had finding a place to stay in the Mediterranean. Now he's found someone to tell about it. Don't let him keep you in the cathedral too long, though, or we'll never get any shopping done."

"Considering the condition of my checkbook after a week in Paris, it would be a good thing." Jennifer leaned forward to observe the narrow city sidewalks which were thronged with pedestrians. "This looks like a busy time—is something special going on?"

"Not really. The stores are closed most of the afternoon, so everyone shops in the morning."

"Then it's absurd of you to waste time sitting around the hospital with me," Jennifer said firmly. "I can meet you at . . ." she broke off, trying to remember.

"St. John's Co-Cathedral, just before noon. It's right in the center of town." The secretary bit her lip and said, "But I told Reed I'd take care of you."

"That's silly." Jennifer leaned forward to tap their driver on the shoulder. "We've changed our plans."

"Well, if you're sure," Louise said, leaning forward as well, to instruct him. "Drop me on Merchants Street before taking this lady on to the hospital, please." She turned back to Jennifer. "You won't have any trouble getting a taxi back to town, and if you're early, you can go shopping, too."

A little later, Jennifer dismissed the cab at the entrance of the hospital's casualty section and was admitted to see the doctor after a short wait.

"You look better," he said, when he'd finished examining her. "Dr. Whitney must have done his job well. He wasn't sure how he'd fare as a night nurse, but I told him not to worry."

Jennifer flushed under the man's amused glance. "He was very kind. I really needn't have bothered you, either—I'm feeling a great deal better."

"Well, don't take things too fast for a day or two. I understand you're leaving on a ship for Egypt tonight." He turned and started to wash his hands while he continued speaking over his shoulder. "Just sit in a deck chair with that young man of yours and enjoy the sunshine. It's the best thing in the world."

"Dr. Whitney isn't my young man—I'm just working for him. But I'll be happy to follow your orders. Every woman I know is looking for a doctor who'll prescribe sitting in a deck chair on a cruise ship."

"With a good-looking man by their side. That's an important part of the treatment. Be sure and tell Dr. Whitney." He helped her down from the examination table. "I'll stop teasing you, Miss Rogers. Seriously, use your common sense and take those tablets at night if you have trouble sleeping."

"Then I can go shopping and sightseeing this afternoon?"

"If you don't try to see all of Malta before you leave."

"I won't. They said something about the cathedral . . ."

He nodded, walking with her to the door. "Couldn't be better. You'll enjoy that. I'm sorry I haven't time to take you myself. Don't miss the tapestries and the Caravaggio." He saw Reed standing by the desk outside and beamed. "There's Dr. Whitney. Miss Rogers didn't mention you were waiting," he went on to the other man.

"She didn't know," Reed said, shaking hands with him. "I was visiting another part of the hospital and thought I'd better come and claim my secretary before you had second thoughts."

"She's all yours," the doctor told him.

Jennifer wasn't sure she approved of that comment and decided to set things straight. "The doctor told me to find a deck chair and a shipboard flirtation on the way to Egypt," she announced defiantly.

Reed's expression didn't change. "Modern medicine never ceases to amaze me," he said. "I'll see what I can arrange."

"I'm sure you will." The older man became serious. "I also told Miss Rogers to use her common sense and not get overtired. I'll rely on you to enforce things."

"Don't worry," Reed said. "I'll make sure that she follows the rules." He gave Jennifer a slanted grin. "Except for the shipboard romance, of course. It's hard to know what the prospects will be."

"I can manage that part very nicely without any help," Jennifer informed him austerely. She softened her tone as she shook hands with the doctor and thanked him.

Reed followed suit and then steered her toward the entrance. "I've already taken care of the bill," he said, reverting to his normal brisk tone. "The receptionist called for a taxi, so it should be parked outside. Where's Louise?"

"I left her shopping in town." Jennifer pulled up before he could open the door. "Wait a minute—you came here checking on Elias, didn't you? Is there anything I can do?"

"Not a thing—there's no reason whatever for you to get involved," Reed reported emphatically. "I'll tell you about it on the way back to town."

"Really, I wish you wouldn't treat me as if I still wore braces and pigtails," she said, staying stubbornly where she was. "I *am* twenty-three years old."

"Do tell." He sounded profoundly unimpressed as he urged her forward. "I can see our taxi and the driver looks restless. You can show me your birth certificate later."

After he'd told the driver where to take them in Valletta, Reed sat back in his corner of the seat, pointedly keeping a two-foot clearance between him and Jennifer.

She waited fully three minutes for him to satisfy her curiosity before saying as reasonably as she could, "You were going to tell me what happened at the hospital."

"Was I?" Reed's tone showed he still wasn't impressed. "Okay, I'll give it to you in that 'adult' version you prefer. I contacted the police in Valletta and they brought me to the hospital to check the victim's personal effects."

"For identification?"

He shook his head. "They'd already taken fingerprints and matched them with their National Service records . . . police records, too. The fellow is Elias Ferrugia—no doubt about it."

"Wait a minute, you're going too fast for me. You mean it was *our* Elias—the one you hired?"

"You don't have to spell it out," Reed said somewhat grimly. "The man in the hospital is *our* Elias, as you put it. He was still wearing the same clothes at the time of his accident that he was wearing when he drove you earlier in the day. The police were interested when I showed them the scrap of his shirt I found in the tower, and they're running a check on the bloodstains now. They can't ask Elias about it because he's still in a coma and not expected to regain consciousness."

Although Reed made his pronouncement in a matter-of-fact tone, Jennifer winced as she heard it. There was a silence between them for another mile. Then finally she said, "I'm surprised that they didn't want a statement from me."

"There was no need. You couldn't tell them anything new, so why drag you into it?"

Jennifer didn't know whether to be grateful or exasperated. After a moment, she chose the latter tack. "Well, really! You might have checked with me first. I don't see why you have to make all the decisions."

"I had the feeling that your family would prefer it that way," he cut in flatly. "After yesterday, I didn't think you should become further involved, especially if that attack on you was deliberate. It would be different if you could identify that man in the tower. Isn't that right?"

Jennifer nodded reluctantly. "I wish I could. I just caught a glimpse of his face, and his robe covered the rest of him. Maybe the regular goatherd could tell the police something."

"No luck. The police have interviewed all the villagers who might have been in the area. Nobody's talking. Elias's friends aren't forthcoming with information either."

"I wonder why?"

"Because Elias wasn't a bosom chum of the gentlemen in blue. He'd tangled with them too recently." Reed took pity on her puzzled face and went on to explain. "The man belonged to one of the left-wing political factions here. Independence from Britain wasn't enough for them; they want their own people in power and will do anything to achieve it. Demonstrations, general strikes, picketing of foreign companies—you name it and Elias was there. The police detained him twice; once for questioning on an illegal break-in and another time when there was a bombing at one of the American-owned textile mills here. Both charges were dropped for lack of evidence."

"If he disliked the foreign elements so much, I'm surprised that he let you hire him with Foundation funds."

"Ours not to reason why . . ." Reed shifted slightly in his corner of the taxi. "The Maltese people have been brought up on a diet of turmoil. I'm not surprised Elias had some decided political ideas."

He bent down to peer through the window at the solid front of limestone buildings on either side of the street as their taxi approached the center of town. That part of Valletta resembled any other European city with traffic jams of small cars and throngs of people. Shops were narrow on the street frontage with stairs leading down to more commodious basement showrooms. At sidewalk level, there were shining brass nameplates on every office door to identify the occupants. Reed sat up again and checked the time. "I'm astounded that Louise didn't stick around this morning. You didn't have anything to do with her decision, did you?"

Jennifer kept her voice casual. "If you mean, did I push her out of the taxi—no. She just mentioned that the stores here closed in the early afternoon and it seemed a shame for her to miss a chance to go shopping. She'd planned to buy some Maltese crosses for gifts." Unconsciously, Jennifer's tone turned wistful.

Reed hid a small smile. "There should be plenty of time for you to buy one before we catch the ferry. The man who runs the jewelry shop in the hotel is an obliging soul—he wouldn't mind opening a little early for a good cause. As a matter of fact, we could use shopping as a good excuse to get away from the rest of the crowd. How about having lunch together and then telling them we've made another appointment."

"No, I can't. I've already made other plans." Her refusal was sharper than Jennifer intended, but she saw no point in hiding her feelings. Just then she was in no condition to withstand the attraction of the man beside her. She had been disturbingly aware of it in Madeira, and meeting him again in Malta had proved disastrous to her peace of mind. Now that they'd shared a bed the night before, his very presence made her quiver with awareness. But physical awareness could be a far cry from love, and if she was going to emerge relatively unscathed when this job was over, she'd need to stay out of his way whenever possible. Otherwise she'd be a sorry case, like the woman that Louise had told her about at breakfast. "I promised the others that I'd spend the afternoon with them," she went on brightly. "Franz and Edwin know all about the history here, so it should be a fascinating experience."

Reed's brows drew together. "Why not buy a guidebook? You don't even have to do that—I defy anybody to get through the cathedral without an 'official' guide gluing himself onto the party."

Jennifer hadn't expected any opposition. "That may be, but Franz is counting on our spending some time together. I can't change things now." Fortunately, the taxi drew up alongside the formidable exterior of St. John's Co-Cathedral and she saw Louise browsing through the contents of a pushcart stall near the steps while Edwin and Franz stayed in the shade by the huge entrance doors. Jennifer hardly waited until the cabdriver had stopped before she reached for the door handle.

"Just a damned minute," Reed snapped, clamping a hand over hers. "It won't hurt them to wait a little longer. What's all this about spending the afternoon with Franz? You just met him yesterday."

"That has nothing to do with it," Jennifer flared back. "Unless you have some work for me to do, I can't see any possible harm in letting

Franz show me around until the ship sails."
Her glance held his defiantly. "*Is* there anything you want me for?"

Reed didn't bother replying to that. He simply gave her a stony look and dropped his
hand, letting her get out of the car. "Go
ahead," he told her in a voice that wasn't particularly pleasant. "I'll be there in a minute."

She hurried to join the others. Just then she
had no desire to continue the discussion with
Reed in his present mood, since he was sounding like the unapproachable employer she'd
first encountered. Her desire to play safe had
boomeranged and from the expression on his
face, she wasn't going to be let off easily.

She and Louise had just joined Edwin and
Franz at the top of the cathedral steps, when
he caught up with them.

"Everybody's right on time," Edwin announced in his precise way. "We can have
lunch first and then Franz can show Jennifer
through the cathedral. I didn't think you'd
want to see it again, Reed."

"It was good of you to remember. Unfortunately, I'll have to skip lunch, too. As I told
Jennifer, I can't spare any time this afternoon."
Reed put up a hand to cup her chin affec-
tionately as he continued, "We can meet for a
drink after we board the ship. In the meantime,
my sweet, take care." No one except the girl
caught in his grasp could tell that the grip of
his fingers was hardly lover-like. "Remember

what the doctor said—after all, you had hardly any sleep last night." His knowing smile made Jennifer's pale cheeks bloom with color, a color which became fiery when he bent down and kissed her in a possessive, lingering way that caused passersby to smile in envy.

Reed was smiling, too, when he finally raised his head. He carefully disengaged Jennifer's fingers from his lapels and stood her upright again. "I'll see you on the ship," he said, "and in the meantime—"

She had to clear her throat before she could get any words out. "In the meantime . . . what?"

His tone was mocking. "Have a nice day."

Chapter Five

After that, the rest of the afternoon could only be anticlimactic. Jennifer did her best to discourage questions and shrug off the impact of Reed's leave-taking, declaring she could hardly wait to try an honest-to-goodness Maltese restaurant for lunch.

Once they were seated in the patio of a popular eating place a few blocks from the cathedral, she encouraged Edwin to display his fund of information about Malta. He complied happily and at great length, recounting how Christianity came to the island when the Apostle Paul was shipwrecked there in 60 A.D. That story lasted through their tasty main course of broiled red mullet washed down by an Italian white wine. When the table was cleared for dessert, he told the legend of how Paul was bitten on the hand by a viper after he placed a bundle of sticks on the fire warming the survivors. "Naturally the Maltese people expected him to die after that happened," Edwin said. "They sat around waiting and proclaiming that since he had escaped from the sea that day, he would suffer fate from another way. When nothing happened they decided he was a pagan god and started singing his praises." Edwin paused in his narrative long enough to admire the saucers of fresh strawberries being put in front of them along with a bowl of coarse sugar and then went on, skipping to a more modern era in the island's history. "The saga of Maltese heroism during World War II is almost beyond belief. The islanders endured more than three thousand air raids before it was over. When Italy entered the war in 1940, the entire Royal Air Force contingent on Malta consisted of three planes," he said, waving a spoonful of strawberries to emphasize his point. "Imagine! Three old Gloster Gladiator biplanes named Faith, Hope, and Charity to protect convoys in 'Bomb Alley.' I'm not surprised Malta won the George Cross in 1942."

"It doesn't pay to tangle with a Maltese even today," Franz told Jennifer as he lounged in a chair by her side. Since Reed's action at the cathedral he had been unusually subdued, speaking only when courtesy demanded it. "There's a saying here that the natives are such sharp bargainers they don't even leave you with your eyes to cry with."

Edwin overheard that as he finished the last strawberry in his saucer. "They probably learned their lessons from the Egyptians. Wait until you try buying something in Cairo. Aren't you going to finish your strawberries?" he asked

Jennifer hopefully, seeing her push the dish aside.

"I can't—I didn't leave room," she said, and then added, "It's a shame to waste them."

"My feeling exactly. I'll finish them for you," he said promptly.

Louise was busy settling her crocheted sun hat more firmly on her curls and paid no attention to the maneuver, but when Jennifer encountered Franz's gaze, she saw his veiled amusement.

He was careful not to show it, though, when he said to the older man, "Probably Reed has already briefed Jennifer on how to bargain in these parts."

"From the way he acted, I think he intends to handle her education personally," Edwin said between swallows, showing he hadn't forgotten the leave-taking at the cathedral either.

"Well, if I can help you in any way, Franz told Jennifer, "just let me know."

"You'd better take him up on it," Louise contributed. "Franz knows this island like a native. Egypt, too."

"Just part of my job," Franz disclaimed.

"That's right." Edwin finished his extra helping and leaned back, patting his solid waistline. "When a man works for me, I insist on the proper qualifications." He gave Jennifer an arch look. "Reed goes about hiring his people in a different way, I imagine." Before anyone could comment, he folded his napkin and directed his attention to his own secretary. "There are some memos I want to get out and I think it's easier to work at the hotel than aboard ship. Those staterooms never have a decent desk."

She shrugged. "Whatever you say. I've spent all my money anyhow. That jeweler I found this morning was a regular Scrooge."

"Probably you would have done better on Fifth Avenue," Edwin told her unfeelingly.

Franz took a final swallow of coffee before asking, "You don't need me, do you?"

"No . . . no." Edwin brushed a crumb from the front of his seersucker jacket as he stood up. "Go ahead and show Jennifer the sights. Louise and I'll use the Mercedes, though. Too bad we're short of transportation."

"Really, Franz, you don't have to take me anywhere," Jennifer protested.

He put up a hand and said firmly, "I've been looking forward to it all day."

Old-world gallantry was the tonic her spirit needed just then. She smiled back at him. "Then I accept with pleasure."

"So that's settled. Take good care of Jennifer this afternoon," Edwin instructed Franz, "we can't have her in any more difficulties." It was impossible to tell whether he was referring to her past problems with the goat herd or impending ones with Reed Whitney, and he went on without explaining. "Be sure and phone my room when you get back to the hotel. Louise and I will be packed by then and ready to go.

We should allow plenty of time to get to the boat."

Franz nodded, saying, "Fortunately, our car ferry is able to tie up at the pier so that will save time." He turned to Jennifer and explained, "The main harbor here is small and busy, so many of the ships have to anchor out by the breakwater. That means waiting for a tender to carry you back and forth."

"I still don't like to rush," Edwin said querulously.

"Don't worry," Louise patted his arm. "You know you can depend on Franz. We'll see you back at the hotel," she told the other two.

It took some time for Franz to settle the check with their waiter, and when he'd finished, Edwin and Louise had disappeared out onto the street. "Let's give them plenty of time to get away," Franz said with a grin to Jennifer. "Otherwise, Ed will think of something else for me to do when I get back to the hotel. Louise had the morning off, so she can handle him this afternoon. We take turns most of the time."

"He does sound like a . . . hard worker." Jennifer's last words were a lame substitution for "slavedriver."

Franz didn't appear to notice. "It's the only way to get ahead with the Foundation. Those of us with European backgrounds approach our projects in such a manner. You've probably noticed that Reed is not enthusiastic about Edwin's methods."

"He's never discussed it," Jennifer could say quite truthfully.

Franz's smile widened as he motioned her toward the street. "And you wouldn't tell me if he had. That's the way it should be. A man has a right to expect loyalty from his . . . secretary."

Jennifer's color rose at his innuendo and she turned to face him. "Dr. Whitney is simply a friend of mine and a good-bye kiss doesn't mean a thing between friends. Americans do it all the time."

His dark gaze rested on her thoughtfully. "I see. I had no idea the custom was so widespread. Do most American employers kiss their secretaries in such a friendly way when they take leave of them?"

"Well . . . it depends." It was hard to tell whether he believed her or not. At any rate, Louise would certainly set him straight if he asked her later on. Jennifer brushed back her hair distractedly and tried for safer ground. "We'd better get on with this sightseeing. Shall we go back to the church?"

"Yes, of course—if that's what you'd like." His voice showed that he would have preferred discussing American kissing habits, but he fell into step beside her. "The co-cathedral is closest, and you shouldn't be walking around outside when you're not used to the Maltese sun."

Since her beige poplin dress was sticking to her back at that very instant and the lightweight material felt like chain mail, she nodded in agreement. They crossed into the next block and went along a now-deserted sidewalk while she asked idly, "Why do you call it a co-cathedral?"

"Because Pope Pius VII raised it to that status. The first cathedral in Malta was the one in Mdina. That's a place up on a hilltop not far from here called the 'old city' or the 'silent city.' It was the capital of the island until they built Valletta. Now it's sort of a mystical, forgotten place with fortifications and narrow streets where the oldest Maltese families maintain ancestral *palazzi*."

"It sounds tremendous!"

"We might have time to get a taxi and drive through it afterward," Franz said, checking his watch.

"Whatever you say. Maybe we should skip this one and go straight there."

"Certainly not." The tour guide in Franz's soul was shocked. "You must see this first. No visit to Malta would be complete without it."

She raised her hands. "I surrender. Lead on and tell me what I'm supposed to know."

Franz took her at her word and started reciting facts and figures, and a little later Jennifer found herself equally intrigued by the surroundings. The co-cathedral was dazzling, with paintings and gilding on every available inch of the interior. Even the marble slabs on the floor added to the magnificence of color, though they served a double purpose as the final resting places for the famed Knights of St. John. At the end of the church, the main altar, of lapis lazuli and rare marbles, glowed softly under stained-glass windows.

Franz led her on to a chapel where a caretaker proudly unveiled one of Caravaggio's last works, "The Beheading of St. John."

"It's not very cheerful, is it?" Jennifer said, trying to restrain a shudder at the grim subject matter.

"The artist wasn't feeling cheerful then because he'd just fled from Rome to Naples to get away from a murder charge." Franz took her elbow and steered her to a stairway. "Come and look at the Flemish tapestries up here. They're based on paintings by Poussin and Rubens and I defy you to not like them."

The tapestries were awe-inspiring, and Jennifer hastened to tell him so. When they finally emerged into the sunshine a little later, her thoughts were pleasantly awhirl with what she'd just seen.

They were lucky in finding a taxi with an English-speaking driver for the ride to Mdina, and it was nice to sit back and let the breeze blow on them through the open car windows as they took the winding road up the hillside. Franz didn't attempt to be overly familiar, but he didn't sit in the far corner of the taxi, either.

It was an effort for Jennifer to keep her mind on what he was saying because her thoughts stubbornly persisted in going back to her earlier cab ride with Reed. Even as Franz was pointing out the walls and gates of Mdina, Jennifer was wondering why Reed had chosen to go off by himself for the afternoon. Fortunately, she was able to keep one ear attuned to Franz's commentary about the Cathedral of St. Peter and St. Paul and nodded at the proper times. When they'd driven through the quiet streets, made even more austere by the shuttered windows on the ancient buildings, he directed the driver to pull over so they could inspect the view from an old gun platform.

"Down there," Franz said, pointing toward a church with a distinctive large dome on the plain far below them, "is the famous Rotunda—the parish church of Mosta."

Jennifer murmured politely and moved over so there was room for their driver on the platform, too.

Franz went on with his tour-guide lecture. "That was the place which featured in one of the strangest happenings of World War II. In 1942, a bomb dropped through the dome, hitting the wall twice on the way down, and rolling completely across the church floor." Franz paused to add a final touch of drama. "There were three hundred people in the church when it happened. Not one was even injured because the bomb didn't explode."

The taxidriver muttered something under his breath and made the sign of the cross before saying, "We didn't know then that we'd be in worse trouble these days. The terrorists wounded three people in a bombing here just last month."

"But why?" Jennifer wanted to know. "What's the reason for it?"

"They want Malta for the Maltese," Franz said. "It's one way of forcing the government to nationalize more industry and give the political minorities more power."

"That's no excuse for violence."

The taxidriver agreed with her. "If people die from a bomb—what difference does the motive make?"

"That may be," Franz said, as they turned back to the cab, "but there's enough political pressure now that the government forces are starting to weaken. At least that's what Edwin thinks. He hears more of the rumors than I do."

Jennifer took time for a farewell look at the old city as the taxi started back down the hill toward Valletta. "It's so lovely and peaceful up here that it's hard to leave."

The taxidriver's glance met hers in his rearview mirror and he nodded soberly. "Most of us pray that one day all of Malta will be like that."

"Just now, it's more important that we don't waste time getting back to our hotel," Franz told the driver. "Otherwise you won't get that tip we discussed."

Jennifer wriggled with embarrassment even though Franz added in a softer tone for her ears alone, "Naturally I will pay him, but he should not be so familiar with his passengers."

"I didn't mind."

"Nevertheless, it is not the custom here."

Jennifer remembered that Elias's manners weren't formal when he'd driven her the day before, and the thought was enough to bring forth a vision of his hospital ward. A frown creased her forehead as she wondered whether he was still among the living. From what Reed had told her, there wasn't much hope. Then she suddenly thought of something else Reed had reported. "A bomb! Or was it explosives?" she murmured.

Franz stared at her in amazement, clearly thinking she'd spent too much time in the sun. "I beg your pardon?"

"Elias was connected with some trouble about explosives. The church at Mosta reminded me of it." Her frown deepened. "I think the police dismissed his charge, though."

"Elias?" Franz was still looking perturbed. "You mean the driver that Reed hired? The one who was taken to the hospital?"

"Of course." She kept her voice low. "We were talking about terrorist groups a few minutes ago. Maybe Elias was connected with them."

"I don't see what that has to do with an accident on a cliff," Franz said. "That sort of thing happens frequently here on the island. You must not be so imaginative. After all, the authorities would explore such possibilities."

"That's what Reed said," she acknowledged reluctantly.

"And from the sound of the newspaper report, it was a straight-forward accident."

Jennifer thought of the bloody scrap of Elias's shirt that Reed had found in the tower, but Franz was going on before she could mention it.

"Undoubtedly the Egyptian papers will carry a follow-up if there's anything to report," he said, "but I should think that you'd be glad to forget it after your accident yesterday. Louise told me how that happened." He tried a heavy attempt at humor, "Unless you feel the goats were politically inspired."

"They didn't stop to apologize so I'll never know."

"Probably because you didn't speak the language."

She smiled at him, glad of a chance to change the subject. "Then I'll buy an Egyptian phrase book on the ship this afternoon. I might tangle with a camel over there and not come off nearly so well."

Their conversation remained on that lighthearted level for the rest of the ride, and Franz handsomely overtipped the driver back

at the hotel. Friendship was cemented by
handshakes all around, and Jennifer was still
smiling over her shoulder when she ran into
Reed's formidable figure just past the revolving
door.

"So you finally arrived," he said in a carefully level tone, all the more frightening by its
restraint. "What in the hell were you trying to
do—miss the boat?" The last was directed to
Franz, who was standing awkwardly by.

"I'm sorry, Reed," he said. "We were caught
in the traffic on the way back from Mdina. I forgot that Jennifer would still have to pack."

"There's no need to make a federal case out
of it," she told them, still somewhat bewildered.
"I can hurry. It shouldn't take me more than
fifteen minutes."

"I'll give you five," Reed announced, turning
her toward the elevators. "The boy will come
up for your bags while I'm checking out. Meet
me back down here when you're finished—and
step on it!"

It was easier for her to take the stairs than
wait for the elevator. Once in the room, she
threw things into her cases with reckless abandon and the bellhop only had to wait a minute
or two when he arrived to pick up the bags.

Jennifer sent him on his way and lingered
long enough to survey her harried reflection in
the mirror. Reed certainly wouldn't approve of
her taking time for repairs. She sighed and
tried to pat her wind-blown hair into order as

she went out the door. This time, she waited for the elevator because her panic had brought on the beginnings of a headache.

Reed probably noticed her pallor because his voice was more controlled as he ushered her into a taxi. "You can catch your breath on the way to the harbor."

Jennifer waited until they were turning out of the hotel drive to say, "I thought we were all going to the ship together."

"There wasn't room in the Foundation car. I told Franz we'd see them on board."

"Oh, lord, I didn't even thank him for taking me this afternoon."

"You'll have plenty of time later." Reed's tone was laconic. "I wouldn't count on any lingering sessions, though. Edwin is a little annoyed at having to hunt for that young man every time there's any work to do."

"But he was the one who insisted on Franz's touring me around."

"Maybe he was pressured into it. Louise fancies herself in the matchmaking role. I happen to know that Franz wasn't around this morning when Ed needed him."

"Why don't you just say that Franz isn't the only unsatisfactory employee on this trip?" she countered just as coldly. "I think it would be better if my salary started tomorrow."

"Would you also like to pay your hospital bill?" he asked with annoyance. "I don't know why you have to act like such an irresponsible

fool. Lord knows, I'm making allowances for
the fact that you're under the weather..."

"That's kind of you."

"... but it still doesn't give you license to
go off on a sightseeing trip just so you can flirt
with the hired help. Frankly, I thought you
had more sense."

Reed didn't disguise his anger, and Jennifer
saw the driver keeping eager track of the argument in his rear-view mirror. She frowned,
making him switch his attention hastily back to
the traffic. Then she turned to the man beside her and said in a tone calculated to annoy
the most dedicated pacifist, "I refuse to provide
a spectacle for the natives simply because you're
suffering from a lack of sleep. You may be able
to browbeat my brother and the rest of the poor
creatures who work for you, but don't try it with
me."

Reed's jaw was so tight that it might have
been carved out of stone like the office building
they were passing. "I'd damn well like to try
something else with you."

She drew back instinctively, banging her
head painfully on the side of the car.

"Serves you right," Reed growled. "Now, if
you've finished reading the riot act, you could
try acting like an adult. I'll even apologize first
if it helps." He looked amused. "I'd hate to
carry you up the gangway kicking and screaming."

She sniffed audibly. "There you go again.

Any other man would have apologized long ago."

"Where would you like me to start?"

"How about the church steps?"

"I thought you'd get back to that. No—don't flare up again. That was simply a means to an end. Louise already had spread the word about our spending the night together, so I decided Ed and Franz might as well respect my boundaries."

"You make me sound like a piece of territory up for grabs," Jennifer sputtered. "Did it ever occur to you that I'm not handing out land grants to anybody? Especially not on a two-week option."

"Well, don't worry about it. My god, I thought last night would have proved that I didn't have any designs on your virtue," he concluded sardonically.

"After what I've learned about your reputation, I wasn't taking any chances.

Her declaration made him frown fiercely. "What in the deuce is that supposed to mean? Anybody would think I had women stacked in closets all around the countryside. There's nothing in my past that you need to worry about . . ." He broke off as their driver pulled to the curb and turned off the ignition. The man was still enjoying their dialogue in the back seat, but there wasn't any place he could drive to prolong it since the cab was already at the edge of the pier. Passengers bustled by, intent on getting their luggage to porters, while a line of cars was being directed aboard the stern end of the huge ferry.

Reed reached for his wallet and told Jennifer, "The important thing now is to get aboard. Wait on the curb while I round up a porter to take care of you and the luggage."

"There you go again." Her tone was bitter. "You sound as if you had requisitioned me for this job along with the typewriter."

"Don't be ridiculous. I have a motto at home that says, 'Never invest in anything that eats or needs painting.'" He opened the door for her. "That lets you out on one count at least. Now just stand over there and stay out of trouble."

Despite her annoyance, Jennifer found herself caught up in the excitement of watching the activity around them on the long quay. Down below there was a fleet of *dghajjes* shuttling across the busy harbor. With their boatmen sculling at the stern, the elaborately carved hulls looked very much like their modern Venetian counterparts. Only the Eye of Osiris painted on the bows identified them as Maltese.

The French car ferry looked like a modern invader in Valletta's Grand Harbor, next to the ancient bastions of Senglea. There was no such distinction, however, between the Maltese passengers waiting to board and their Mediterranean neighbors. The women showed an Italian fondness for the latest fashion just like the French passengers, who had clearly enjoyed a stopover on the island. From the good-natured conversations around her, Jennifer concluded that the rest of the passenger list was a potpourri of nationalities. There were Germans, fair-haired Scandinavians, Italians by the score, and a few businessmen whose skin tones and language placed them in the Middle East.

She turned to comment on it after Reed gave their stateroom number to a ship's porter and came to retrieve her. "I think we're the only Americans around. That's certainly a switch from Paris," she said, her previous annoyance forgotten.

He appeared in a better mood, as well. He nodded and reached over for her tote bag. "This is a little off the tourist trails. European car ferries are generally for the locals. We'd better get aboard though—it's almost sailing time."

Jennifer walked beside him toward the end of the gangway. "When you said car ferry, I thought you meant the small size. This could double as a cruise ship." She was staring at the gleaming white vessel, which showed a promenade deck above the car storage area and awesome rows of stateroom portholes. Even the crated cargo lashed on the bow didn't detract from the ferry's sleek outline.

"There's lots of traffic around the Mediterranean at this time of year." Reed paused to hand a steamship official their passports and tickets, receiving two stateroom keys in return. He thanked the man and followed Jennifer on up the steep gangway. Once they'd reached the top of it, he consulted a deck plan. "We go one more deck up and then down to the right."

Hearing the babel of French around them, Jennifer made a wry face, as she climbed a flight of carpeted stairs in the center of the ship. "I might as well be back in Paris again—I didn't understand anything there either."

Reed led the way down a narrow corridor with stateroom doors on either side. "Don't worry—Ed and Franz are fluent enough and I can get by."

"What about Louise?"

He shrugged and pulled up in front of a door amidships. "She's never far from Edwin, so it doesn't signify."

"I gathered that at lunch. I'm not sure if he knows it though." She followed Reed into a small but immaculate outside stateroom with a single bunk against the wall and pulled open the blue-and-white print curtains covering two portholes before inspecting an adjoining bath. "This looks fine . . . where's your cabin?"

Reed took a deep breath. "This is mine." He walked beyond the bath to another door. "I thought you'd prefer being in here."

She moved slowly across the room and peered around his shoulder. "It's just like this cabin except"—her eyes narrowed and she stared accusingly up at him—"there's no other door. I'd have to come through this stateroom."

He raked a hand through his hair. "Yes, but you can close the door the rest of the time. This is classed as a 'family' unit so the kids can be fenced in, I guess. There wasn't anything else available when I made the reservation. Frankly, I didn't give it a second thought. There were two beds, and I knew your brother wouldn't give a damn about the layout."

Jennifer nodded, aware that Jeremy's absence was still causing repercussions and Reed could scarcely be blamed for them. She decided that she'd make this new complication as painless as possible. "I'll take the inside one, then. We'll have to work out a schedule so that you won't feel like you're living in Times Square."

Her calm acquiescence surprised him. "Oh . . . that," he deposited her tote bag in the cabin, keeping scrupulously to the middle of the threshold. "I don't plan to spend much time down here, anyhow. Here's your key for the hall door. The luggage should be along any minute. I think I'll wander around on deck until we're clear of the harbor." He ran a finger inside his collar, although the air-conditioned temperature in the stateroom was a balm after the hot sticky air on the pier. "Just for the record—you won't have to worry about any hanky-panky. That kiss on the church steps was . . ."

"Strictly for effect," she cut in, keeping her

tone matter-of-fact. "You've already made that clear, so we can forget about it. It's time I started earning my salary, though. That dressing table is about the right height for a typewriter."

"I guess so, but the doctor told you to take it easy. Tomorrow will be plenty of time to do any reports."

She stared at him strangely. "Well, if you're sure. It doesn't sound as if you even need a secretary on this trip."

"If I didn't, you wouldn't be here." His manner was brusque again. "Come up on deck when you feel like it. I promised we'd all meet for a drink before dinner."

"Where will you be?"

He grinned then. "With the rest of the crowd. Remember, this is a French ferry." As the vibration of the engines showed that they were sailing on schedule, he opened the hall door. "Time to put this place behind us, I can't say I'm sorry."

She still stood in the middle of the cabin when he'd gone, letting emotion show on her face for the first time. Then she walked slowly over to stare through the porthole for a last glance at the Grand Harbor of Valletta. She pressed her forehead against the cool glass as she thought about all the people who'd tried to storm the bastions of those rugged limestone cliffs, looking so drained of color in the unrelenting rays of the afternoon sun. Only the blue of the Mediterranean was unaffected until the white wake of the ferry surged against the breakwater in a sudsing froth. Then they were past the boundary and leaving the island behind.

She bit her lip and tears suddenly trickled down her cheeks when she remembered Reed's last words. The worst part was, she couldn't blame him for the way he felt. Memories of their stopover in Malta weren't the kind for pasting in a scrapbook. All that had happened was that she'd turned out to be a plaguey nuisance, and fallen in love with her boss in the bargain. Jennifer smiled bitterly when she recalled her attempt to classify it as mere physical attraction. That was rationalization of the first order.

Her hand went up again to mop her wet cheeks while she considered the future. Now she had two days on the ship plus three more in Egypt before the drama concluded. She'd already discovered that a one-sided love affair was pure hell, but at least she had her pride still intact. With any luck, she'd keep it that way.

Chapter Six

Jennifer's decision would have been simpler to enforce if all the elements had cooperated.

There hadn't been any trouble the first night. She'd joined the others for cocktails, but immediately after finishing dinner in the modern dining salon with its square windows along one side, she pleaded weariness and retired to her cabin early. By the time she heard Reed enter the outer stateroom, she had turned off the light and was in bed behind her closed door.

He must have tried not to disturb her because other than a few muffled sounds there was nothing to mark his presence, and she fell asleep while the sliver of light still showed under their common door.

The next day, she barely waited until after breakfast before she started typing, and she used a lengthy report on Africa's resource development as an excuse to have lunch in her stateroom. Around the middle of the afternoon, Louise came down to insist that she enjoy a half hour of sun beside the swimming pool where most of the passengers were congregated. Jennifer agreed reluctantly, but the weather deteriorated and made a perfect excuse to leave early. That brought forth an immediate protest. Even Edwin, looking uncharacteristically relaxed at a table shaded by a canvas umbrella, insisted there was no need for her to work so unstintingly. "Look at those two," he went on, waving his glass of beer toward the bronzed figures of Franz and Reed lounging in swim trunks nearby. "They haven't done a bit of work all day. Even Louise absolutely refused to stay down in the cabin." He bestowed a fond glance on the older woman, who'd limited her sun attire to slacks and a sleeveless blouse.

"It was stuffy," his secretary replied complacently, putting up a hand to make sure that her hairdo was still unruffled by the slight breeze. Her expression was provocative as she turned to him. "Besides, I met the Radio Officer when I was prowling around the boat deck after lunch and he told me that the weather prospect isn't good. That's why I thought we should all enjoy the sun while we could."

Reed had evidently been listening, because he opened his eyes to survey the sky and sat up reluctantly. "Damn! I thought the wind was kicking up. How much of a storm are we in for?"

"You know how ship's officers are. They don't admit anything's wrong until they're pushing you into a lifeboat. Not that it's going to be anything like that," she added hastily as Edwin scowled. "It's just that they have to stay on schedule or they'll lose their docking privileges in Alexandria. They can't lower speed just for the passengers' comfort."

"And car ferries roll even in a flat sea." Reed addressed Jennifer for the first time since she'd appeared on deck. "Better make sure that you take a motion-sickness pill before dinner." With that, he turned over on his stomach and closed his eyes again.

Jennifer contented herself with a frown in his direction. Even the realization that she was in love with the man didn't blind her to his irritating manners. Franz was interested in getting a suntan, too, but he'd supplied her with an iced drink and seen that she was comfortable after she'd come on deck to join them. Just then he looked up and intercepted her glance.

"You look unhappy," he said softly. "Does the thought of bad weather worry you?"

"No . . . it wasn't that . . ."

"Good." Franz stubbed out his cigarette in a ceramic tray on the table and added, "There's no need to be. This is one of the newest ships on the Mediterranean—but I suppose Reed has already told you."

"No, he didn't mention it," she said to him. "I'm glad to learn that I can relax, after all."

Ed's assistant cast another look at Reed's motionless figure and leaned closer to say, "If you had time, I'm sure I could arrange a visit to the bridge before dinner. We've traveled with this captain before and he's very obliging."

Jennifer waited, certain that Reed would react somehow to Franz's newest proposition. She wasn't disappointed; he did stir and get leisurely to his feet. "Looks as if the sun has disappeared for good," he commented without rancor as he reached for his towel. "There's no point in my hanging around. See you at dinner."

Louise stared after him and then turned back to the rest of them, "What a gift that man has for conversation! I'm surprised he doesn't charge by the word."

"There's nothing personal in it," Edwin soothed. "It's common knowledge at the Foundation that Whitney likes to work alone. Not everybody is gifted with the same social graces." His tone showed clearly that he considered himself one of the fortunate ones.

"Reed has plenty of charm when he chooses to use it," Louise argued. "Every woman at the main office will tell you that."

Edwin sat up straighter in his canvas chair. "That's simply Foundation gossip—something that every bachelor on the staff has to contend with. Just ask Franz," he said, with a nod toward the younger man. "There've been plenty of rumors about him."

"All without basis," Franz assured Jennifer hastily. "And nobody could find fault with a visit to the ship's bridge. Even Reed didn't object—so you will come, won't you?"

"Yes, thanks. I'd love to. Now I'm going below before I freeze in this wind." Jennifer stood up, and rubbed her arms briskly. "What time shall I be ready?"

"Probably just before dinner would be the most convenient time. I'll call you in your cabin after I've checked with the officer on the bridge."

Jennifer didn't hurry on her way back to the stateroom because she wasn't anxious to tangle with Reed in case he'd changed his mind. Since he'd objected so strongly to Franz's squiring her about before, it was unlikely he was going to let this invitation pass completely unchallenged.

Fortunately, when she reached the stateroom door, Reed's cabin loomed emptily before her. The bathroom door was swinging partly open with the increasing motion of the ship, but she peered around it to make sure the room was unoccupied as she walked through to her cabin.

This time, she left the connecting door between the rooms open—merely to show Reed she was still at work, she told herself.

Franz's call came a little later. "We won't be able to stay up on the bridge long," he cautioned. "Apparently this weather is turning out to be worse than they expected. I've told Ed to go on in to dinner without us, if we're delayed.

Want to meet me at the forward elevator in half an hour?"

"Sounds fine to me."

"I'm glad that you're still feeling all right," he went on. "Louise isn't interested in eating tonight. You must be a better sailor."

"The motion hasn't bothered me yet, but I'll take a pill right now to be sure," Jennifer replied, surprised that she hadn't noticed how the stateroom curtains were swinging as the big ferry moved into the storm.

She was in the bathroom swallowing the motion-sickness pill when she heard the corridor door open. Closing the medicine chest carefully, she went out to find Reed, fully dressed, putting his key on the bureau.

"Where did you change clothes?" she asked impulsively.

Reed's eyebrows climbed. "There's a gym and conditioning department aboard—complete with lockers and saunas. Why? What difference does it make?"

"Not the slightest, I assure you . . ."

"Oh, not that again." He sounded thoroughly weary of her protestations. "You'd have a better disposition if you stopped going steady with that damned typewriter. Why don't you go out and get some fresh air?"

She started for her cabin door. "That's exactly what I have in mind. I'll change for dinner before I meet Franz, and there'll be fresh air on the way up to the bridge."

Reed had been lounging against the end of the bureau, but he straightened abruptly. "You mean that idea is still on?"

"Of course, why not?"

"The weather—that's why not," he snapped. "Did Franz check with the officer on watch?"

"Just five minutes ago." Her nonchalance was marred by having to clutch her cabin door to stay upright. "He has official approval. And if the Captain doesn't object, there can't be anything wrong with the idea."

Reed walked over to the bathroom door before commenting drily, "Nevertheless, I'd make your visit short and sweet. The officers have plenty to do in this weather besides amusing passengers."

"Such as?" She kept her voice unconcerned.

"Such as making sure that everything's secure down on the car deck and that the cargo on the bow is still with us."

"Why wouldn't it be?"

Reed jerked a thumb toward the cabin's portholes where the spray could be heard hitting the glass even if it couldn't be seen in the dark. "There's a considerable wind out there." When he saw her sudden anxiety, he relented. "You don't need to worry. The only way passengers get in trouble in weather like this is by doing something stupid. So don't try jogging to the dining room or surf fishing from the rail."

She smiled. "That wasn't on my schedule."

"Then there's no cause for concern, is there?" he said, and closed the bathroom door.

His stateroom was still deserted when Jennifer emerged to meet Franz a half hour later. In deference to the weather, she'd put on shoes with a chunky heel and had dressed for dinner in a pleated challis skirt and blouse topped for the moment by a nylon raincoat. It was an informal combination, but she doubted that many women aboard would bother about fashion in the rough weather. The raincoat was a last-minute decision, since she wasn't sure whether the bridge tour would all be under cover.

She was forced to walk carefully down the corridor to avoid losing her balance when the ferry wallowed between waves. A passing stewardess, carrying a tray of tea and dry toast murmured an absentminded *"Bon soir,"* her mind clearly occupied with the list of passengers who had decided to remain in their cabins rather than face food in the dining salon.

In the big empty foyer near the elevator, Franz was leaning against the wall watching a crewman cordon off the area with rope. "Something for passengers to hold onto," Franz explained to Jennifer when she approached. "A narrow hallway is one thing, but large, open foyers are another."

"And the rope serves as a makeshift grab rail?" she murmured.

He looked puzzled at her terminology and

then agreed, "That's correct. Now, are you ready to go?"

She nodded, noting that he was carrying a raincoat over his arm. "I wasn't sure whether we'd get wet or not. It looks as if we will."

"Depends if they take us out on the wing of the bridge." He was pushing the elevator button impatiently as he spoke. "We don't usually have to wait this long."

"Maybe the elevators aren't working properly in all this motion. Why don't you ask that fellow?" she urged, nodding toward the crewman who was still stringing ropes onto stanchions. "I'd rather not take any chances. Getting stuck on an elevator in the middle of the Mediterranean is too horrible to contemplate."

Franz gave the button a final annoyed punch and then decided to do as she asked. The conversation that followed was in rapid French, but when the sailor shook his head and shrugged, it didn't need much explanation.

"He doesn't know what's wrong," Franz finally told her.

From the way the crewman was glaring at him, Jennifer felt that it wasn't an exact report on the interchange, but she didn't pursue it. "Well, we can always take the stairs," she said instead. "Which way do we go?"

Franz made an exasperated gesture. "Passengers aren't allowed on the forward stairs to the bridge—especially female passengers. You'd have to go through the Officers' Quarters."

She put out a hand to steady herself against the elevator door. "Damn! Does that mean the tour is off?"

"Not after all the trouble I had setting it up. There's an outside stair at the bow that leads up to the bridge from this deck." He ran his glance over her. "Have you a scarf to put over your hair?" When she nodded and pulled one from her raincoat pocket, he said, "Do you mind if we detour outside?"

"Whatever you say." She started tying the plastic rainscarf over her hair. "I wouldn't like to spend the night out there, but a little rain won't hurt us."

"That's the spirit." He shrugged into his raincoat and took her arm as the crewman muttered something else over his shoulder. Franz's answer was short and pithy. He didn't comment on it to Jennifer, simply urging her down the stateroom corridor toward a door near the bow. "We go out this way. I'll try to hold the door for you, but hang onto the stair rail when you get outside. The deck will be slick in the rain."

As soon as Jennifer edged her way around the door which he shouldered ajar, she found that his warning was a gross understatement.

It was doubtful, however, if anything could have prepared her for the wall of rain which deluged her when she stepped outside. She instinctively put up a hand to shield her face and struggled for balance as the deck slanted beneath her feet. The big ferry was finding it heavy going through towering waves which thudded against the hull. Even as Jennifer looked toward the railing and the black sea beyond, another cloud of spray cascaded over her, drenching her legs below the hem of her raincoat.

She took one careful step toward the stairs and then another while Reed's warning flashed through her mind: *"The only way passengers get in trouble . . . is by doing something stupid."*

Then the unwieldy vessel shifted again as the bow submerged and the propeller cleared water at the stern. A heavy slithering sound came through the tumult in the murky darkness, and Jennifer hovered by the stair rail trying to identify the cause until a flash of light flickering over the lashed deck cargo showed that a heavy wooden crate had broken free in the storm. An instant later, the same light caught her figure in the edge of the beam.

"Aufpassen!" someone shouted from the ship's bow. Another voice joined the commotion, crying *"Vite, vite, mam'selle!"* But it was the roar of "For god's sake, girl—move!" that sent her ducking behind the steel stairway just as the crate crashed into the railing where she'd been a moment before.

After that, it took only seconds before Franz and Reed were pulling her to safety under the covered part of the deck. At the same time, a trio of crewmen in oilskin slickers swarmed up to secure the crate against the crumpled stair railing. Jennifer caught a final glimpse of their frenzied activity before Reed shoved her back through the heavy door to the companionway. When he got her inside, he took a deep unsteady breath. "If this is how you go on, I'm not surprised your brother was in the hospital. Are you sure it wasn't for a nervous breakdown?"

"I don't blame you for being mad . . ."

"My good girl," he flexed his fingers, "I'd like to strangle you here and now."

"That's strange, since you just went to so much trouble to save my neck," she said, trying not to show how reaction was making her knees tremble.

"You mustn't blame Jennifer," Franz interjected. "I should have been out there with her. If I hadn't got my coat caught in that blasted door handle, I would have protected her."

"Never mind—I heard you shout at me," Jennifer said, hoping to make him feel better. "I heard everybody shouting except that I didn't understand . . . until Reed used English. Now I'll have to get changed again. I can't go anywhere looking like this."

"Nor I." Franz glanced down at his soaking trousers and shoes. "I'll phone the bridge to say we aren't coming. Better still, I'll go up and explain what happened. I'm sure Reed will escort you back to your cabin."

"Don't worry about it," Jennifer said. "I'll see you at dinner."

Reed didn't comment on that until Franz had made a fast exit down the stateroom corridor that connected with the interior stairway to the bridge. Then he turned back and motioned for Jennifer to precede him through the foyer with the rope guides. "Why in the hell didn't you take this elevator up to the bridge?" he asked as they came to the shaft.

"We tried, but it wasn't working." She flushed as the elevator doors opened just then and a couple stepped out. They nodded and tactfully averted their glance from her sodden appearance when they passed by. "Well, the elevator wasn't working when Franz tried it before. If you don't believe me, you can ask the crewman who was stringing the ropes."

He ignored that to say instead, "What was wrong with the inside stair? The one Franz used just now?"

"It passes through the Officers' Quarters and they don't allow women visitors there." As he raised a skeptical eyebrow, she added, "Well, not officially. I don't know what the rules are otherwise."

"All right—I can understand that. Then why didn't you call off the whole idea?"

"Because I didn't know there was such a storm outside. Franz didn't either. We didn't think that we'd have any trouble."

"You didn't think—period," he said, not hiding his annoyance. "That's no surprise, but frankly I expected more of Franz. I'll take care of him later," he said, pulling up at the stateroom and reaching for his key. After unlocking the door, he ushered her through. "I'll start running your bath water while you get out of those clothes."

"There's no need for you to make such a fuss," she protested.

"No? Then you haven't looked in a mirror lately."

His brutal assessment brought tears to her eyes, and she was fumbling fruitlessly for a handkerchief when she felt him push one into her hand.

"Use this, for god's sake." His voice was just as stern, but there was a strange undercurrent to it—almost as if he'd been stretched to his limits, as well.

After mopping her eyes, Jennifer watched him go and turn on the bath water. When he had it adjusted properly, he straightened and paused for a moment to wipe his hands on the nearest towel. In that unguarded interval, she saw that his face looked tired and vulnerable— probably from having to watch over his secretary around the clock. Jennifer decided the kindest thing she could do was stay out of his sight for the rest of the evening. "I think I'll get into a warm robe after my bath and have dinner in here," she announced, trying to sound as if the idea really appealed to her.

"That's the first sensible thing you've said all day. I'll tell the stewardess to come with a menu in about half an hour. Just one more thing—I'll spread the word to Franz that you're not receiving any company. That way you won't be tempted to make any more mistakes tonight."

Jennifer's face grew even paler as Reed's sarcasm registered. "With all your extracurricular activities I'm surprised you can find time to do any work," she flared.

"I manage to fit it in," he said ominously.

"Well, you can stop worrying about me. My biggest mistake was agreeing to come on this trip in the first place."

"And I was a damn fool to ask you, so we can change the subject." His words came out like wedges of ice. "Now take off those wet clothes and get in that tub. Otherwise, I'll have to take care of that for you, too, which would be an even bigger mistake." He paused to let his masculine glance rake deliberately over her, not missing a curve in the appraisal. "The way I'm feeling now—you wouldn't approve of my methods."

Chapter Seven

By the next morning both storms had abated.

The Mediterranean had settled down to an expanse of gentle swells with only the salt-caked glass on the portholes remaining as evidence of the storm's fury.

Jennifer wasn't sure about the tempest that had raged inside the cabin until she reached the dining salon and sat down at the breakfast table. Edwin and Franz greeted her calmly, but Jennifer held her breath until Reed looked up and added his "Good morning" a moment later. His guarded expression showed that he hadn't forgotten the argument, but he wasn't going to prolong the unpleasantness.

After Jennifer had given her order, she looked around the sun-lit dining room. "I'm glad they're opening the drapes so we can enjoy the view again. Do they always close them during storms?"

"I should think so," Edwin said in his precise voice. "It doesn't aid your digestion when the waves are going over the porthole next to you. The waiters had a terrible time even trying to get the plates to the table, so it was just as well you skipped dinner here. I must say—you don't look any worse for the weather. Louise is still feeling ill this morning." There was a discreet silence before he hastened to add, "I stopped by her stateroom on the way here."

Franz looked slightly haggard as well, although he was immaculately dressed in a dark gray suit and tie. "Something must have worked the miracle for you," he said to Jennifer. "You look very nice wearing that shade of green."

"At least my dress is the only thing that's green this morning," she said lightly. "When we finally got off that deck last night I felt green all over. Did they ever get that crate of cargo secured?"

"Right after we left," Franz said. "The Mate apologized for the inconvenience."

"Decent of him," Reed looked up from his plate briefly. "I'm glad that he didn't have to visit Jennifer in the hospital to do it."

"I agree with Reed," Edwin put in with a severe look at his assistant. "It was an unnecessary risk, and you're both fortunate that you weren't injured. The weather can be deceiving on this crossing—I can remember a time when our sailing was held up for half a day from Alexandria because of high winds."

"At least the weather should be good until we reach Egypt this afternoon," Jennifer ventured, hoping for a more cheerful conversation with her toast and egg. She looked across at

Franz, who had the ship's bulletin beside his plate. "Does it say whether we'll dock on time?"

He surveyed the notices casually. "They don't say that we won't—that must mean something. Want to see it?"

"No, thanks. My French isn't good enough for translating news items."

"I'm surprised they don't have an English version," Edwin put in. "Louise was complaining about the emergency instructions on her cabin door. Apparently the first alarm is given to passengers in French, followed by an English version. After that, all instructions are given only in French."

"It's just as well I didn't see it," Jennifer said. "Or better still that we didn't run into any emergency. I'd have even been tearing around the deck looking for a translator."

Reed's stern expression lightened. "That could have taken a while with this passenger list. The English-speaking souls are few and far between."

"It wouldn't bother you," Franz told him. "Your French is very creditable, from what I've heard. Now, if you'll excuse me—I have some things to do in my cabin. Would you like your news bulletin back?" he asked Edwin, getting up.

The older man shrugged. "It doesn't matter."

"I'd like to see it, if you're finished," Reed said, reaching across the table. "It seems to be the only way of getting any news while we're on board. The radio reception was terrible when I tuned in last night."

"There isn't much in this. Mostly headlines and sports scores," Franz said, handing over the bulletin. "I'll see you all at lunch."

After his departure, a silence fell over the table. Edwin was concerned with getting another order of toast, and Reed appeared completely engrossed in the news sheet. The first intimation of anything wrong came when Reed uttered a soft, "I'll be damned!" from behind the mimeographed page.

"Undoubtedly we all will," Edwin said, annoyed that his waiter was proving elusive. He turned back to Reed. "Now what's wrong?"

"The news from Malta," Reed lowered the ship's bulletin to frown at him. "Did you read the notice?"

"I didn't have time this morning. What's all this about Malta?"

"The terrorists have surfaced there again. Unless the government meets their demands in the next forty-eight hours, they're threatening more bombings."

"What kind of demands?" Jennifer asked.

"It doesn't say. You know ship's news sheets—they just pick up summaries from the wire services. This isn't even one of the lead items." He folded the paper and handed it back to Edwin with a preoccupied air.

"Chances are they want the release of some

political prisoners," Edwin said, his attention back on his breakfast.

"Elias!" The name was out before Jennifer thought.

"That taxidriver?" Edwin sat up straighter. "What does he have to do with it? I thought he wasn't expected to live."

"I don't know if he did." Reed managed a warning glance at Jennifer. "There isn't anything in the news about it."

Edwin wasn't to be diverted. "Then why would he be associated with the terrorists? Wait a minute . . ." His brow furrowed. "I remember now! Franz said that he had a police record. He was connected with a bombing attempt in Valletta once before, wasn't he?"

"They couldn't prove anything," Reed replied. "The charges were dismissed for lack of evidence."

"Nevertheless, this gang might want him out of police custody if there's a chance of his recovering. Maybe he knows too many people for them to rest easy. Of course, it's all conjecture." He shrugged negligently and picked up his coffee cup. "I've learned to stay out of internal wrangles when we're in these countries. That reminds me, when are you going to make your official calls in Cairo? It would look better if we appeared together—to present a united front from the Foundation."

"I suppose so." Reed didn't sound enchanted at the prospect. "When do you want to go?"

"I hope to secure an appointment first thing tomorrow morning. That way, no one can be offended. Franz can make the arrangements." Ed looked distracted suddenly. "Our transportation to Cairo could be a problem. There isn't room for more than four people in the Mercedes—not with any comfort in the afternoon heat. And I promised Louise a place . . ." His words trailed off apologetically.

"Don't worry about it. Jennifer and I will share another car," Reed told him. "How about the hotel reservations in Cairo?"

Edwin was glad to be able to reassure him. "No trouble there. I had Franz doublecheck before we left Malta—five single rooms as we requested. That's right, isn't it?"

"Absolutely," Reed replied drily.

"It took some doing, I can tell you. Cairo hotels are always full." Ed cast a regretful look at his still-empty toast plate and pushed back his chair. "It's time I checked with Louise to see if she feels like working this morning." He paused by Reed's elbow. "I don't suppose Jennifer would have any time . . ."

"That's right," Reed said without embellishment. "She won't have any time."

Edwin didn't look surprised. "I've found that it never hurts to ask," he commented before going out of the dining room.

"Pompous idiot!" Reed said. He reached over to pour more coffee from the porcelain pot on the table. "If Louise had any sense, she'd have found a replacement for Edwin long ago."

"Nonsense—they deserve each other." There was an instant's pause before Jennifer added, "I don't like it."

"What? Doing extra work for Ed? I don't blame you. Let me know if he tries again . . ." he broke off as she shook her head.

"No, not that," she said. "As a matter of fact I'm almost finished with your report. I wouldn't have minded."

"Well, I would—so don't start volunteering," he announced, his chin jutting ominously. The silence between them lengthened until he went on. "I suppose you're referring to last night— well, maybe I was a little rough on you. Not that you didn't ask for it."

Jennifer's expression wasn't encouraging. "If that's the best you can offer for an apology, you'd better try again. At least Franz or Edwin wouldn't . . ." She started over when she saw Reed's eyes narrow angrily. "Sorry, I'm not doing much better, am I?"

"Let's forget about Franz and last night." Reed lounged back in his chair. "Now, what is it you don't like this morning? You can't object to five single hotel rooms in Cairo?"

She smiled slightly at his teasing. "Not in the least. I was beginning to think there weren't any in this part of the world." Her expression sobered as she went on. "I meant that I didn't like that news item from Malta. Could Elias be connected with the terrorists?"

"Your guess is as good as mine. We won't be able to find out anything until we dock this afternoon and get a European newspaper. Maybe you can buy one on the pier while I'm hiring a car to take us to Cairo."

"Will it be difficult? The car, I mean."

"Shouldn't be. There's usually a taxidriver who wants to earn American dollars for a long-distance fare." Seeing her puzzled expression, he added, "It's a long drive from Alexandria—three and a half hours in a good car. Keep your fingers crossed that we're on time docking. Otherwise, it'll be after dark when we reach Cairo."

"I didn't realize it was so far."

"That's because you didn't spend enough time with a geography book when you were in school."

"You're right. Cairo sounds fascinating, though. Will you have to work all the time we're there?"

"It depends on what statistics the government authorities have assembled. I set up some guidelines when I was here before, but it's difficult to evaluate what effect Aswan Dam is having on their ecology in a short time. We know it's affected the flow of silt along the Nile, almost ruining the sardine industry of the country. Unfortunately, the new water conditions have affected people, too; there's been an increase in a disease acquired by contact with the infected waters. We want to find out how bad the problem is and try to correct it." There was a thoughtful silence following his words. Then he made an apologetic gesture. "Sorry, that's more of a sermon than I intended."

Jennifer waved that aside. "I had no idea. Then you're going to confer with the officials taking the survey?"

"Mostly. The Foundation just acts in an advisory capacity, and it's difficult because there's more than one government agency involved. For example, one set of officials checks aquatic vegetation, but they have to cooperate with another set of officials trying to improve the sanitation along that same stretch of the Nile." Reed put his napkin on the table. "There won't be any work for you to do while I'm involved in these meetings, so you might as well act like a tourist."

Jennifer's eyes shone with enthusiasm. "Do you mean it?"

"Certainly I do. Even if we were busy, you'd be entitled to play hooky. There's nothing to compare with your first sight of the pyramids rising from the desert at Giza."

"It sounds fabulous! I wish you could come, too."

"So do I," he said, sounding as if he meant it. "Unfortunately, this is one time that Edwin's right. There's no way I can avoid those meetings tomorrow morning. Unless it was a matter of life or death, and we left that behind in

Malta—thank god." He stood up and pushed his chair into place. "C'mon, I'm taking you back to the cabin."

"What for?" she asked, but obediently swallowed her coffee and got up beside him.

"So you can change into shorts or a swim suit and get some sun on deck."

"But there's still work to do." Her objection wasn't as emphatic as it should have been, and his amused look acknowledged it.

"Then you can bring a pad and pencil along," he said, motioning for her to precede him from the almost-vacant dining salon where waiters were resetting the tables for lunch.

"But I can't take shorthand," she confessed. "I only had six months in high school, and even then I had to write it down in longhand to catch up."

"Who said anything about dictation? If you have to be doing something, I'll give you a list of places to visit in Cairo tomorrow."

She smiled up at him without any attempt to hide her delight. "I was wrong earlier."

"How's that?"

"When I said that you didn't know how to make an apology."

He rubbed the back of his neck, clearly at a loss for words. Then he admitted wryly, "In that case, I'll stop while I'm ahead. Go change your clothes and I'll snaffle a couple of isolated deck chairs. I've never claimed to be psychic but, the way things have been going, I have the damnedest feeling that we should take advantage of this interlude. There's a line of Browning's where he says something about 'Outside are the storms and strangers.' Let's keep it that way for this morning at least."

"Good enough." Jennifer's voice was noncommittal. "I'll go and get changed."

She kept her expression suitably demure until she rounded the corner of the corridor out of Reed's sight. Then she surprised a passing stewardess by taking the stairs two at a time and swinging happily on the newel post when she reached the next deck.

Reed should have picked another secretary if he wanted to keep his inner thoughts to himself. Either that, or choose one who didn't like English literature. As if any woman could forget Robert Browning's immortal poem, "Never the time . . . and the place . . . and the loved one all together. . . ."!

Reed hadn't really committed himself, she decided, trying to be strictly impartial. He had chosen two lines and then stopped abruptly. But when a hard-headed scientist like Reed Whitney started quoting Victorian poets at ten-thirty in the morning, it was a start in the right direction.

Chapter Eight

The big car ferry was precisely on schedule arriving at Alexandria that afternoon, but the passengers didn't need a timetable to tell that the fabled port city was in the offing.

Jennifer was by Reed's side at the rail as they started passing the phalanx of freighters anchored three miles offshore waiting for berths at a pier. When Jennifer commented on the number, Reed nodded and said, "Be thankful passenger vessels have a priority. Some of these ships will still be waiting out here next week. It's not bad for the crews, but I imagine the owners are crawling on the ceiling." He raised a pair of binoculars to survey a vessel a good distance from them. "I'm wondering about the registration on that rustbucket over there. Looks Panamanian to me."

Jennifer was happy that his preoccupation with the ancient freighter gave her a chance to study his lean figure unawares. That afternoon he was dressed in light-weight gray slacks and a short-sleeved sport shirt that showed a powerful breadth of shoulder while still leaving a great deal to the imagination—unlike many of

the European men on board who affected outfits that strained at every seam. Reed's waist
and hips could have borne scrutiny, but most
of the male passengers who followed the continental styling should have been following a
good diet instead. She let her glance wander
up to Reed's profile and found him staring
steadily back at her.

"What's got you looking so sleek and satisfied?" he wanted to know.

"Nothing special," she prevaricated, hoping
he'd think her heightened color came from the
temperature. "I'm excited at being so close to
Egypt. Look—you can start to see the buildings
of Alexandria in the distance." She frowned as
she stared more closely. "What's that haze
above them? It seems to cover everything."

"Smog, or a combination of dust and factory
smoke—you name it. Once we get off the water,
it'll be hot, too. I approve of your outfit." He
made no attempt to hide his leisurely glance
over her halter-topped sundress. "If you visit a
mosque tomorrow, though, you'd better choose
something that's not quite so bare."

"You make me feel as if I'm in a bikini," she
protested, glancing down over the green linen.

"Simmer down—that's not what I mean.
There's nothing wrong except the sleeveless
part and the sort of"—he gestured with a big,
tanned hand—"scooped-out back. I know it's
tame by Fifth Avenue standards, but here in
this part of the world, the women have just

dropped their face veils, and they have a long way to go." He suddenly noted how Jennifer was struggling to keep a straight face. "You know exactly what I mean, my girl. If you don't watch out, I'll turn back history and carry you ashore all rolled up in a carpet."

"My textbook never mentioned what Cleopatra was wearing under the rug. From what I recall, though, she had some other assets beside a brilliant mind."

"So have you," Reed grinned. "And tomorrow, make sure that they're discreetly covered."

"Yes, sir, Dr. Whitney, sir."

As their laughing glances met and held, a current of awareness flared between them which was as strong as the teak railing at their side. Jennifer's heartbeat thundered and Reed finally had to take a deep breath before saying in a voice far rougher than usual, "Anyhow—remember what I said." He sounded as if he was making a determined effort to get his thoughts under control again. "We should be docking in another hour. There's the pilot boat coming out to meet us."

Jennifer wasn't sorry to change the subject herself. For the next half hour, while they carried on a desultory conversation about the minarets on the hazy city skyline and crowded harbor conditions beyond the Alexandria breakwater, part of her was still going over that magic moment by the rail. For an instant, Reed had shed his austere manner and looked as if he wanted to take her in his arms. If he had, the kiss would have been far different from the one he'd used as an object lesson on Malta.

Outwardly, Jennifer matched Reed's effort to concentrate on the scenery. The big ferry was nudged through the busy city harbor by two of the dirtiest tugs she had ever seen. They couldn't claim that distinction alone, because the color of the harbor water exactly matched their bilious shade of brownish-green. When the tugs reversed engines as they edged up to the pier, the mud from the harbor bottom made the water look even worse.

Jennifer mentioned it. "That reminds me of the warning they put on cigarette packages. You know, about being 'detrimental to your health.'"

"Don't you forget it," Reed said. "Egypt is the prime example for the traveler's golden rule, 'Cook it, peel it, or uncork it.' Otherwise, you'll be laid out with 'Rameses' Revenge'— more popularly known as 'King Tut's Tummy.'" When she started to giggle, he shook his head, "It's no joke, believe me."

"I'll be careful, I promise," she said, sobering.

They stood watching as the lines were made fast at the bow and the stern and a few minutes later, a forklift edged the main gangway into place. Behind it, an elevated concrete ramp led to a modern terminal building which serviced the tourist part of the pier. The contemporary structure was the new Egypt, but an old man in a burnoose who was sweeping a loading platform with a twig broom looked as if he'd lived in the time of the Pharaohs.

Reed noticed it, too. "You'll see the contrasts all over Egypt, especially on our ride into Cairo. The people are still using farming methods that date back to Cleopatra. At least I hope you'll see them," he added, checking his watch. "This docking is taking a lot longer than I thought it would."

"Edwin was worried about making the drive after dark, too." She chuckled suddenly. "I'll bet the three of them are already down in the car waiting to drive off the minute we've tied up."

"Maybe I should have pulled rank to get you a ride into Cairo along with them. I have a feeling that the transportation we can hire won't be as elegant as the Mercedes."

"If you'd pulled rank, Louise and I would have been left thumbing a ride by the roadside. Frankly, I prefer it this way."

"So do I. Don't look now, but I think they've finally secured the gangway. We'd better go down and corral a porter for the luggage and head for the taxi stand in front of the terminal."

Jennifer nodded as she took a last look at the steady stream of Egyptian men coming up the gangway. Most of them were in immaculate Western clothes and wore badges from tourist agencies in their lapels, but the porters following them were in shirts and baggy pants which had seen better days. All of them wore Arabic fezzes and their faces were shiny with perspiration.

When Jennifer followed Reed and two porters laden with their suitcases down the gangway fifteen minutes later, she could understand the Egyptians' wilted appearances. The late afternoon heat of Alexandria felt like a blast furnace when she stepped onto the broad concrete ramp leading to the terminal.

It was a busy place, with a large Italian cruise ship tied up at the same pier and a Norwegian vessel getting ready to sail across the way.

When they finally reached the big building housing shops and banking facilities, its shady interior made it difficult to see and Jennifer groped for Reed's hand as they approached a wide marble stairway leading to the street below.

"Take it easy," he cautioned, gripping her firmly. "We're not in *that* big a hurry."

Even after her eyes adjusted to the dimmer light, Jennifer had trouble concentrating because there were so many things to see.

Tourists of every nationality thronged the terminal and most of them lingered by the merchandise displayed all around the edges of the big room. There were brass boxes and trays heaped on the floor in careless array along with camel stools and wall pieces of embroidered Egyptian cotton designed to catch the travelers' eyes. What drew Jennifer's fascinated gaze were the rows of stuffed camels cleverly constructed from fur, ranging in height from twelve inches to four feet.

A look of mock horror spread over Reed's face as he followed her glance. "Now look here," he said, "there's no way that I'm going to share the back seat of a taxi for three hours with one of those furry things."

"But they're darling!" she breathed. "I've never seen anything like them."

"With good reason. How many people want a four-foot camel standing around in a three-room apartment?"

A wicked gleam came over her features. "Jeremy might. Sort of a get-well present. And if he didn't want it . . ."

"You could keep it. I'm beginning to understand how your mind works. Look—I'll make a bargain with you. You can buy your camel when we're leaving the country, although you'll probably have to carry him on your lap in the airplane."

"That doesn't matter."

He grinned at her prompt response. "Better you than me. When you do buy one, it'll have to be sprayed."

"What for?"

"To get rid of the rest of the livestock living in that fur. That's why I'd rather you didn't buy one now."

She nodded reluctantly. "But I'd still like to get one before we leave."

"Fair enough. When that time comes, I'll help you choose it. You can window-shop now while I go outside and try to negotiate for a cab."

"What about the luggage?"

"I'll keep it with me." He gave a harried look around the busy terminal. "Somewhere here there's a newsstand selling English papers."

"I'll find it. You go ahead," she said briskly, turning away from the camels so she wouldn't be tempted. "There should be a follow-up on what's happening in Malta."

"I hope it's something good." His tone was that of a man who didn't expect to find anything particularly cheerful in the headlines. "There's always a first time."

It took longer to track down a newsstand than Jennifer thought and involved going back up the stairs again to another part of the terminal. The foreign newspapers were tucked away behind the counter of a curio shop, but the owner understood enough English to pull out *The Egyptian Gazette* and assure Jennifer that it had just arrived from Cairo. She paid him with American dollar and received a handful of grimy paper *piasters* in change.

When she returned to the front of the terminal and found Reed waiting on the curb, she exhibited the tattered currency gingerly. "I think these *piasters* should be put in isolation and fumigated along with the stuffed camels."

"I can find a better use for them right away," he said, taking them from her. He walked over to bestow them on a uniformed man who was directing the port traffic. When Reed came back he told Jennifer, "I'll pay you later. I'd run out of change for tipping and that fellow's arranged for a taxidriver who'll take us into Cairo. He should be here in another five minutes. Incidentally, I saw the others drive off—Franz said he'd like to buy you a drink at the hotel when we arrive."

"And what did you tell him?"

"That I'd relay the invitation but we might be very late," Reed reported without a change of expression. "I see you found a newspaper. What does it say?"

"I haven't had time to look," she confessed, handing it to him and then proceeding to stand on tiptoe and read over his shoulder.

The front page was devoted mainly to Egyptian happenings, but as soon as Reed turned to the inside section, she saw a four-column headline: "New Crisis Threatens in Malta."

"This is it!" Reed muttered, as he scanned the news story beneath. "Damn! It says the terrorists have exploded one bomb, damaging a foreign-owned textile factory on the outskirts of Valletta."

Jennifer was trying for a better look. "Was anybody hurt?"

"A watchman was injured, but he's expected

to recover. The terrorists claim this attack is simply a warning that they mean business. They're demanding that ten political prisoners held by the Maltese authorities be released and given transportation to Libya or Algeria within twenty-four hours."

"I don't see Elias's name listed among the political prisoners. There's no mention of him at all." Jennifer raised a worried face. "Does that mean he's dead?"

"Of course not. We don't even know that he's connected with this extremist group. Or, it could mean that if he's still alive, he's decided to cooperate with the police." Reed shoved his sunglasses farther up his nose. "The authorities aren't even speculating on what the next bombing target will be. Probably don't want to cause a panic." He sounded as if he were simply thinking aloud. "I imagine they've already put guards on the cathedrals and palaces. It must be a hell of a job to try and outguess a bunch of fanatics."

Jennifer made a murmur of agreement, her attention mainly on the bottom of the newspaper where another towering oil rig was pictured being brought into Malta's Grand Harbor for repairs. The accompanying news story cited how island workmen were also completing repairs on an oil-disaster-control vessel owned by British and American companies.

Reed noticed her preoccupation with the

story. "That repair work is certainly a shot in the arm for Maltese economy."

Jennifer frowned fiercely, trying to think. "Elias wasn't happy about it. We saw one of those rigs in Pretty Bay when he drove to the tower that day. He was carrying on at a great rate about the foreign interests on the island." She caught her breath and clutched at Reed's arm. "Foreign interests! They're the common denominator in the whole thing."

She had his full attention, despite the noise and confusion of taxis pulling up to the curb and a truck causing a minor traffic jam near the pier. "You're right about that," he confirmed. "It was a foreign-owned company that was bombed when Elias was implicated the first time."

"And another foreign-owned textile factory in this second attack," she said excitedly. "So why should they change tactics on the next one? This maneuver has probably been planned for a long time, and I'll bet Elias was pressed into delivering some kind of explosive that day I arrived. He turned white as a sheet when he looked in his trunk at the airport. I'm sure he was connected with the terrorists, Reed."

"The police must have thought the same thing—that's why they were keeping such a close watch on him in the hospital."

Jennifer's face was tense with conviction. "But if Elias didn't tell them anything, they still don't know where to expect the next bombing attempt."

Reed's dark brows were an ominous line across his forehead. "What in the devil are you getting at?"

She folded back the paper and thrust it under his chin. "The oil rigs! Don't you see? They fit all the qualifications. Right now the oil question is the biggest political football between the East and the West. The government forces in Malta need the oil revenues to balance the budget and stay in power at the next election. If these fanatics bomb the repair facilities, it would make the oil companies look for a new location to maintain their equipment. The terrorists can't lose—if the authorities bow to their demands, the prisoners are freed, and if they don't"—she made a graphic gesture—"poof! The terrorists have won a political battle."

"My lord, I think you're right. At least it's sure as hell worth mentioning." Then Reed seemed to remember where they were and added, "That isn't easy. In this part of the world, there aren't any pay telephones on the corner."

Jennifer nodded grimly. "The only place in the terminal that might have one was the tourist office on the upper level, but it's locked. I think it has been for weeks. and even if we found a telephone and knew enough Arabic to get through, who could we call in Malta at this time of day?"

"Our best chance is calling from the American Embassy in Cairo tomorrow morning. I know some of the people there, and there'll still be time before the terrorist deadline."

A sudden feeling of misgiving made Jennifer bite her lip and confess, "I could be all wrong about this—I'd hate to have you blamed afterward."

"Who cares about blame? It's certainly worth a try. Right now the important thing is to get to Cairo," he broke off abruptly as he saw the terminal traffic officer motioning them toward an ancient car pulling up to the curb. Reed closed his eyes and then opened them again, clearly hoping that the vehicle would have disappeared in the meantime.

Instead, the middle-aged driver was opening his door and coming around the battered hood to address them. "You want to go to Cairo?" Without waiting for an answer, he made a sweeping gesture toward the car. "I take you. Come in, p'liss."

"Hold on a minute." Reed put out a detaining hand when Jennifer would have obeyed. "There must be a mistake. Let me go talk to the fellow who arranged it." Then, to the driver, "You wait here. I'll be back."

The man nodded calmly and, together with Jennifer, watched him dodge through the traffic out into the middle of the pavement where he accosted the port official. That unfortunate man was trying to move two local drivers who had parked in front of a curbside jewelry merchant, thereby ruining his business. Both the jeweler and the drivers were screaming epithets across the radiators and making gestures that didn't need translating even from twenty feet away.

The traffic official seemed glad to exchange crises, and listened to Reed with a suitably interested expression. At the end, however, there was no mistaking the shaking of his head or the regret on his face.

Reed didn't bother to explain when he returned a minute or two later. He merely said, "No soap. It's this car or wait until tomorrow morning. None of the other drivers want the long round trip at this time of day. This fellow won't get back in Alexandria until way after midnight. If then," he added ruefully with another look at the twenty-year-old chassis of the taxi. "I'm sorry as hell about it. I should have insisted on our joining Ed and the others."

"Honestly, I don't mind," Jennifer told him. "It won't be the first time I've ridden in a car like this."

"Yeah, I know, but the ones at home have a horseless carriage license."

They were watching the driver hurriedly storing their bags in the car's trunk, and the cloud of dust that came up each time he put one in made Jennifer wonder what her suede-trimmed luggage would look like when it came out.

"If you'd rather, we could take the train," she

offered finally when she saw Reed wincing at the driver's repeated attempts to latch the rusty trunk lid.

Reed shook his head and motioned her into the back seat of the cab. "No way. That's worse. I'll show you what I mean when we get on the road." He managed to close the car door behind him on the third attempt. When the driver got in, he leaned forward to tap him on the shoulder before he could start the engine. "You understand English?"

"A leetle. We go to Cairo—you pay American dollars. Yes?"

"That's right. You take us to the new Magreb Hotel—it's near the Hilton on the same side of the Nile. Do you know where I mean?"

Clearly the driver didn't, but his shrug was unworried. "We find. Now we go. Okay?"

Reed wiped his palm over his face wearily. "Okay, we go."

The cab started with a roar that sent blue exhaust smoke billowing behind them, and they lurched off in a way that would have made an automotive engineer clutch his brow. Reed gave a stifled groan before he sat back. "At least the guy in charge said that this fellow was honest and there's lots of traffic on the road if the engine gives out."

"Stop being so pessimistic. We'll make it. Compared to some of my brother's old jalopies, this is going first class." Jennifer had opened the window to let the air blow against her face

in hopes of finding a cool breeze. "Did you ever
see so many people?"

She gestured toward the bumper-to-bumper
traffic on the street in front of them and the
surging groups of people on the sidewalks.
Some of the pedestrians were in Western dress,
but many retained the traditional burnoose and
fez. Donkey carts mingled with automobiles on
the roadway, the animals appearing unfazed by
the shouts and the honking horns around them.
The car drivers treated the donkeys with similar unconcern, skimming past them with just
inches to spare.

The port city looked prosperous, with blocks
of well-stocked shops and plenty of customers
to go with them. Fabric stores were the most
prevalent, closely rivaled by attractive fruit
stands which displayed oranges, limes,
bananas, and tangerines in mouth-watering array.

As their taxi approached the outskirts of the
city, the Western-style clothing gradually was
replaced by ankle-length garments on both
women and men, while the small boys were
outfitted in a cotton pajama-like outfit.

"They look as if they're dressed for bed," Jennifer said, noting a group of youngsters cavorting by the roadside.

Reed shook his head. "You're wrong about
that. They're on their way to bring the animals
in from pasture now that it's starting to get
dark. From here on, we'll be traveling through

farming country." There was the whistle of an approaching train on the track paralleling the highway, and he broke off until the coaches passed.

Jennifer looked in amazement at the passengers jammed into seats and spilling over between rail cars. A few even more daring ones were clinging to the tops of the coaches.

"That's why I didn't think you'd want to go by train," Reed finished drily.

Jennifer was still staring after it, as if unable to believe her eyes. "Good lord, do the ones on the roof ever fall off?"

"Frequently. The authorities discourage roof-riding, but you'll see it on nearly all the trains."

"And to think you were worried about our chances in this splendid automobile." She patted the cracked vinyl seat between them and tried to ignore the broken spring that she was sitting on. "The engine's running fine." Just then, the driver braked and pulled over to the side of the road. "Oh, oh," Jennifer said ruefully, "Maybe I spoke too soon."

"I don't think so." Reed was peering out at a check station staffed by uniformed men. "This is another kind of trouble."

The driver confirmed it a minute later. "Soldiers," he said, getting out. "I go tell them I drive Americans. You have passports?"

Reed offered them through the window.

The other took them solemnly. "Okay, I come

back soon." He walked in leisurely fashion over to the barricades.

"Why here?" Jennifer wanted to know. "Out in the middle of nowhere?"

"Over there is the Nile," Reed said, looking amused at her naiveté. "Those things going down the middle are freight boats called *felluccas* carrying goods from Egypt's biggest port to their biggest city. It's an important artery—so is this highway." When she still looked mystified, he said, "The Israelis, my girl."

Jennifer grimaced. "I should have known."

"If you lived in this part of the world, you would have. Recently the Egyptian authorities dropped a depth bomb in the harbor at Alexandria just because somebody saw some bubbles coming up in the water."

"Good lord, what happened?"

"False alarm," he reported laconically, "but I imagine there were some surprised fish. We must have passed muster, too. Here comes our driver and he's all alone."

The man grinned cheerfully at them, handed back the passports, and said, "We go. No pictures."

"Absolutely," Reed agreed, and they started off again unmolested. "Fat chance of taking any pictures," he went on in an undertone to Jennifer. "It's getting too dark anyway. I'd rather be doing this in the daylight."

She nodded in agreement as the taxi jounced through a rough spot on the surface of the road. The two-lane highway expanded to four lanes separated by shrubbery every once in a while, but there was so much cross-traffic in the farming communities that there was a constant blasting of horns from both sides of the arterial.

One-story mud dwellings with towering dove-cotes on the flat roofs were the standard Egyptian farm homes they passed. Next to the adobe houses, lofty stacks of straw provided fodder for the animal enclosures where the families' donkeys, goats, and cows were teth-ered.

Most of the flat pasture lands between the villages were green with the spring cotton crop. Other small holdings showed sugar cane and orange trees, with the citrus crops protected by a windbreak of straggly pine trees alongside the road. In a corner of the farms, a blind-folded bullock hitched to a crude wooden yoke would be plodding around a hard-packed dirt circle to bring water from the main irrigation canals into the fields.

At every break in the shrubbery, small chil-dren riding donkeys, leading camels, or herd-ing gaunt cattle would start across the road with scant regard for safety. The Egyptian drivers apparently counted a near-miss as a sign of their proficiency and, before long, Jen-nifer was cowering on the seat.

A new menace developed as darkness de-scended; she discovered that the heavily laden trucks and trailers seldom had red stop lights on the back, apparently trusting in their size to provide warning.

After a few devastating encounters, Reed, who looked none too happy himself, decided to try and cheer her up. He cleared his throat and began to solemnly recite,

"There once was a lecherous crocodile
Who lived by the banks of the River Nile."

Jennifer stirred with interest, and stopped back-seat-driving long enough to stare at him. "A limerick?" she asked.

He misinterpreted her interest and said hastily, "Yes, but it's a clean one." Then, as he remembered the punch line, he added, "Oh, hell! I'd better skip it after all."

About then, there came a squeal of brakes when the car directly in front of them decided to make a left turn without bothering to signal. Reed's jaw was at an ominous angle when he leaned forward to tap their driver on the shoulder and said, "For God's sake, man, slow down!" As the driver stared blankly back at him in the rear-view mirror, he said, "Understand? Slow—slower—slowest . . ." The driver obligingly speeded up, and Reed raked his fingers through his hair. "Damn it—no!" He turned back to Jennifer. "What's another word for 'slow'?"

She tried to think and at the same time, ignore the truck they were passing at fingernail length. "How about 'no fast'?" Before Reed could try it, she clutched at his arm. "Good lord—he's driving without lights!"

"What the hell!" Reed's hand descended heavily on the man's shoulder. "Turn on those lights!"

There was no telling whether it was the tone or the words, but the man shrugged and obediently flicked the light switch.

"Now, keep them on." Reed ordered him ominously before sinking back against the rear seat cushion. He reached over and pulled Jennifer's taut figure against him. "Go ahead and close your eyes. There's no use in both of us having a nervous breakdown." When the car swerved onto the soft shoulder of the road momentarily, he said, "It wouldn't hurt to pray a little, too."

She sagged against him, too tired to do anything else. "I've been doing that ever since we left Alexandria."

"Then we shouldn't have any trouble." His arm tightened comfortably. "Besides, this fellow's a downy old bird—he could probably drive this road in his sleep."

She stiffened. "For heaven's sake, don't give him ideas."

"Sorry. Maybe I'd better finish that limerick, after all."

The combination of the dreadful joke, Reed's soothing voice, and keeping her eyes closed, eventually worked the miracle. The next thing

Jennifer knew, Reed was softly shaking her awake and they were stopped in front of an imposing skyscraper hotel. It didn't need his "We're here," for her to recognize that they were in the middle of Egypt's fabled capital.

Beyond the curving hotel drive there was a steady stream of traffic on the streets despite the lateness of the hour. Like their counterparts in Alexandria, every driver seemed to have one hand on the horn along with one foot on the accelerator. Jennifer shuddered, but managed to climb stiffly out of the old car when a uniformed doorman approached.

In her still-groggy state of mind, the modern foyer of the hotel was indistinguishable from similar lobbies all over the world. It took Arabic signs over the elevators and on the branch bank alongside the reception desk to make her start feeling the difference. A party of men wearing traditional white robes and headdresses secured by black corded _iqals_ wandered by her in the direction of a casino. Another group murmured in Arabic as they checked airline schedules by the porter's desk— just as if it weren't nearly midnight.

Reed found her standing near a marble pillar in the middle of the lobby when he came in from paying the cabdriver. "I'll register for both of us," he said. "It shouldn't take long. Here's a paper I bought at the newsstand. It might help you stay awake for another five minutes." He grinned and thrust it at her.

Jennifer managed a sleepy smile in response and leaned against the pillar as she stared obediently down at the paper. It was a later edition of the one they'd seen in Alexandria and her bemused expression faded as she read a short article at the bottom of the front page.

Reed found her still staring at it when he came back with the room keys in his hand. "As soon as we corral the luggage we can go right up," he was saying before he frowned and asked, "What's the matter?"

She pointed to the paper. "It says here that Maltese authorities have announced the death of a key witness from the terrorist gang. It was a suspected member who had been hospitalized and the police had been hoping he could identify the gang leaders." Jennifer looked up at Reed and steadied her voice. "It has to be Elias. Even if you call Malta in the morning and tell the authorities what we suspect, there's no chance of confirmation now." She closed the paper despairingly. "Unless you can think of something."

Reed shook his head wearily. "Not one damned thing," he said finally. "I thought Elias was going to make it. Talk about lousy luck."

She nodded and followed him over to the bank of elevators.

The doors of the nearest one opened just then and a diminutive operator nodded to Reed. "Welcome to Cairo, sir," he said. "Hasn't it turned out to be a fine evening, after all?"

Chapter Nine

It was late the next morning when the volume of traffic noise below Jennifer's sixth-floor hotel room finally penetrated her slumber.

She opened her eyes and stretched in the big double bed that took up most of the space in her modern room and then winced as she turned over. The hotel's furniture and decor might be new, but the mattress felt as if it had been stuffed with old *piaster* notes. When she'd tumbled into bed the night before, she had been too tired to care, but nine hours on the unyielding surface made her feel as if she'd been sleeping in a gravel pit.

The clamor of the city traffic from the street made her remember where she was, and she hastily caught up a robe and padded barefoot across the room to step out on her balcony.

The wave of warm air that greeted her showed that it was going to be another scorcher of a day but, a few blocks away, the broad gray waters of the Nile looked even more exciting than the hotel's modern swimming pool beneath her window. There was a stone bridge spanning the river and four lanes of honking cars occupied it to capacity. A white-gloved policeman in an elevated control tower was doing his best to keep the traffic moving.

Jennifer peered over her railing to see if the pyramids might be visible, too, but found that her balcony faced the wrong way. She moved back into her air-conditioned hotel room then, carefully closing the door behind her while she decided that a trip to Giza would be first on her sightseeing list. At that moment, the phone on the bedside table rang shrilly, and she hurried over to answer it.

Reed's voice came over the wire. "Jennifer? Are you okay? You sound a little strange."

"I'm fine," she reassured him. "I just woke up. I didn't mean to sleep so late."

"That's all right. I have some good news and I wanted to catch you before you went out. I've been in touch with the Embassy, and they got through to the police in Valletta. Elias isn't dead! He's still very much alive, and cooperating in the bargain." A rattle of static came over the telephone wire, almost obscuring his last words.

"That's wonderful! Did you ask them about the oil rig . . . oh, damn!" By then, the interference on the wire sounded like popcorn in Jennifer's ear. "Reed, can you hear me?"

"Just barely." He was obviously shouting into the phone, but there was so much static on the line that she could scarcely understand him. "I'll tell you everything at lunch, okay?" he said, and rang off.

Jennifer stared at the receiver she was still clutching in her hand and then banged it down in annoyance. So much for modern conveniences! The exultation she felt at hearing Elias was still alive was tempered by not knowing whether her suspicions about the oil rig were valid. Of course, Elias might have supplied that information as well. She glanced at her travel clock and raised her eyebrows. Reed must have started early to have accomplished so much by midmorning. If she wanted to do any sightseeing before lunch, she'd have to get moving as well.

Before stepping in the shower she corralled a hall maid and, through gestures, showed that the telephone wasn't working properly. The woman nodded when Jennifer gave her a room-service menu marked for the continental breakfast and indicated fifteen minutes on her watch.

The tray arrived just after Jennifer had donned a short chambray caftan in blue with crisp white embroidery around the neckline and on the long sleeves. The dress was loose and comfortable for hot weather, but would still be acceptable if she wanted to visit something like the Mohammed Ali Mosque.

Breakfast took only ten minutes, and she drank her second cup of coffee on her balcony, drawn by the sights and sounds of downtown Cairo.

A little later she was checking to make sure

she had her wallet and, at the last minute, she tucked a brimmed cotton sun hat in her purse before leaving the room.

The hotel lobby was busier than ever, with patrons thronging the reception desk and standing in line at the bank for money-changing. The porter's cubicle had luggage deposited all around it while hotel guests arranged transportation and late checkouts. Egypt might be short of many things, Jennifer decided on her way to the lobby entrance, but there was no scarcity of foreign visitors.

The cars rolling up the drive to discharge new arrivals ran the international gamut, with the latest American models vying with expensive German ones. Jennifer stood at the top of the entrance steps, wondering if taxicabs were allowed to enter such a sanctified atmosphere, when a small-model Mercedes drew up beside her and Franz signaled from behind the wheel. "You look as if you need a lift," he said, giving her an admiring glance. "Could I volunteer?"

A feeling of relief swept over her and she bent down to address him through the open window. "At least you can point me in the right direction. I only have a couple hours, but there are so many things to see I hate to waste any time. Could I get up to the big Mohammed Ali Mosque and back here by lunchtime?"

He pulled at his ear. "I suppose so. Is that what you want to do?"

"I'd rather see the pyramids at Giza, but I

know there isn't time for me to arrange a trip there," she admitted ruefully.

"I have a better idea. How about coming to the pyramids at Sakkarah with me? There won't be as many people, and we could make a quick trip of it."

By then the big hotel doorman was approaching, intent on clearing the drive. Jennifer opened the car door hastily. "Sakkarah will be fine," she said, and gave the doorman an apologetic smile as he closed the door behind her.

"He was too big to argue with," she confided to Franz once they'd left the hotel and found an opening in the lane of traffic headed for the bridge. "Are you sure this won't interfere with any of your plans? I thought you'd be meeting the planning officials this morning, along with Reed and Edwin."

He shook his head. "It was postponed at the last minute."

"Probably because Reed wanted to make an early visit to our Embassy," she said, trying to explain. "Sort of a last-minute thing."

Franz frowned at that, but after an instant he made an obvious effort to regain his customary good humor. "Well, if our bosses can't get organized, we might as well take advantage of the spare time. You'll enjoy this drive," he added, turning left on another busy highway at the end of the bridge. "We follow the Nile most of the way and you'll see Egyptian agriculture at its best."

"Sounds wonderful," she said, inspecting the interior of the Mercedes. "And in comfort, too. After our taxi ride from Alexandria, I didn't ever plan to get in a car again. Is this the one you brought on the ferry?"

He nodded with some embarrassment. "I'm sorry you had such a bad experience last night. Reed was telling Edwin this morning that we'd have to work out another schedule for transport."

"I didn't know you'd seen him."

"I didn't, but the shock waves from his explosion reached me very shortly," he added in a sour tone. "It wasn't my fault that Edwin and Louise couldn't be separated for the drive yesterday."

Jennifer decided it was a prudent time to change the subject. "Where *is* Louise this morning?"

"Shopping, naturally." His tone was still bitter. "That's what she always does in her spare time."

Either he was sulking from another slight or he hadn't had enough sleep, Jennifer decided, and suddenly wished that she'd gone sightseeing on her own. She turned to watch the passing scene through the car window, determined not to let Franz's sour disposition spoil her morning.

Within another mile, the crowded neighborhoods and buildings of downtown Cairo had thinned to scattered one-story adobe dwellings on small acreages. A man was repairing the palm-frond roof on one of the houses while his assistant approached, leading a camel who was loaded with more fronds to complete the job.

The farmlands looked richer than any she'd seen before, with acres of glossy-leaved citrus orchards. In this area, rows of prickly pear cactus were used to mark boundaries next to the road. Graceful eucalyptus and jacaranda trees provided shade for the inevitable groups of children who were watching their elders work, the little girls with plaited hair, in ankle-length print dresses, and the boys looking like Wee Willie Winkies in their pajama outfits.

None of the farm people seemed to be working very hard. "Which isn't surprising, considering the temperature," murmured Jennifer, thinking aloud.

Franz caught enough of her comment to nod, his own face shining with perspiration. "That's why there won't be many people at Sakkarah," he said. "The pyramids at Giza are crowded all the time because they're so close to the city. It's better to go there early in the day."

"I'm sure you're right." She shifted on the seat and wished that shorts and halter tops were the accepted fashion for foreign visitors. "I hate to confess my ignorance," she went on, "but I've never heard of . . . Sakkarah, is it?"

"Then you don't know much about Egyptian history," Franz said, not bothering to be diplo-

matic. "Sakkarah is near Memphis, which was
the Old Empire's capital city. Probably the
name came from Sokar, who was the regional
god of the dead at that time. We'll only have
time to visit the pyramids this morning, but
later you must see the Alabaster Sphinx and the
other treasures of Memphis." He half-turned to
point through the corner of the windshield.
"Now you can see the famous Step Pyramid—
the tomb of King Zoser. That's worth the journey, don't you think?"

Jennifer bent forward to look and drew in
her breath in delight at the rugged outline of a
pyramid situated on a plateau just beyond the
valley. "It's fabulous! Can we go up there?"

Franz nodded and turned from the main
road along a dirt track that led past palm plan-
tations where young herders sat in the shade as
their goats and thin cattle searched for food.

As the car neared the edge of the valley,
other smaller pyramids could be seen on the
sandy plateau whose barren surface was in
sharp contrast to the lush valley land beneath.

"How many pyramids are there at
Sakkarah?" Jennifer wanted to know.

"There are four near the big Step Pyramid,"
Franz related. "One for King Teti, two for
Userkaf and Unis, and finally the newest discovery called the Horus Sekhem-khet Pyramid
for the king who succeeded Zoser."

"I had no idea you were such an authority
on all this."

"It's of no consequence as far as the Foundation is concerned. They employ me as a secretary—the same category as Louise." His tone showed what he thought of that.

So much for equal rights, Jennifer decided, pulling the conversation back to a safer tack. "I can see why they call it a step pyramid," she said. "There are four of them . . . steps, I mean. They must be huge."

"It was to have been even bigger. King Zoser's vizier, a man named Imhotel, was the man responsible for the construction. He wanted a monument which would resemble a flight of stairs going to heaven—to make it easier for the dead king's soul to ascend to his father Re." Franz turned to add pointedly, "Re was the Egyptian name for the sun."

Jennifer's cheeks took on an added tinge of warmth at his mocking tone. "I *did* know *that*," she pointed out quietly.

When they reached the top of the plateau and drove the few hundred yards remaining toward a barrier surrounding the nearest pyramid, she frowned uneasily. "There isn't another soul around. I can understand why there aren't any visitors here in this heat, but I thought there'd be guards or officials."

"They come on duty later," Franz said, pulling up at the end of the track and shutting off the engine. "There's not much chance for vandalism on the outside of a pyramid."

I guess you're right." Jennifer reached for a

handkerchief to mop her forehead, wishing the slight breeze hadn't disappeared when the car had stopped. "Is there anything more to see if we get out?"

Franz was opening his door. "Certainly—the very best part. There's a tunnel down into the newest pyramid. It isn't officially open to visitors, but a friend showed it to me a few months ago."

She opened her door but hung back. "You're sure it's all right?"

"Perfectly. I was even shown where the officials store the lanterns and working clothes. The tunnel's not far from here, and you'll enjoy the change in temperature once we get down below. It will cool us off for the ride back to town."

"You've convinced me." Jennifer clambered out and hurriedly put on her sun hat once she'd closed the car door. "Lead the way and I'll follow. This is just like being on the beach," she added, getting a shoeful of sand on the first step.

"We'd better hurry. The sooner we're in the shade the better," Franz said, starting out in a hurried walk.

Jennifer tried to keep up, but after a few feet had to make her own pace behind his bobbing figure. The glaring heat made her thankful for her sunglasses, but even with a minimum of clothing and a brimmed hat, she was glad to round the corner of the big step pyramid and find Franz standing by an inclined passage. He was busily putting on a wrinkled burnoose over his shirt and lightweight trousers.

"To keep off the dust," he explained, seeing her eyebrows go up. "There's another one in the storage cabinet if you want to wear it."

The thought of an added layer of clothing made her shudder. "No, thanks. My dress is washable . . ." Her words trailed off as she watched him pick up a flashlight he'd evidently found in the supply cabinet, as well. "Is that all the illumination we'll have?"

"This should be enough," he said, starting down the incline. "Sometimes they leave a lantern in a corner of the chamber. There's only one decent hieroglyph to see, anyhow. Come along, will you?"

Jennifer hesitated a moment longer and then shrugged with resignation. She started carefully down the inclined passage, thankful for the wooden wedges which had been inserted at intervals to keep the sand from filling in the passageway. As soon as she reached the edge of the pyramid beyond the worship temple, the descent steepened and the light grew progressively dimmer. She could barely see Franz's figure ahead of her when he turned and came back to guide her with the flashlight for the rest of the way.

"I'm sorry. I didn't realize you were having difficulty," he said, catching her arm in a firm grip and directing the beam of light onto the bottom of the incline. "We're almost there. Feel how much cooler it is?"

"Uh-huh." Jennifer wished she could sound more enthusiastic, but even the clammy chilled air didn't aid the uneasy feeling in her stomach. "Flash that light around, will you," she asked once they'd reached the end of the tunnel. "I'm not very keen on underground funeral chambers even if they're refrigerated."

"This is perfectly safe." Franz sounded scornful but he did as she asked. The round beam of the flashlight showed a forbidding rectangular chamber constructed of dressed stone, completely empty except for a few workmen's tools left in a far corner. The ceiling was barely above Jennifer's head and it was only Franz's slight height which kept him from stooping as he walked across to a far wall, his footsteps echoing with a hollow sound in the dead air. "Come over here," he instructed her. "This is the hieroglyph I was telling you about."

Jennifer followed reluctantly, the sand grinding unpleasantly beneath her own shoe soles on the stone floor.

"Do you know anything about the symbols used by the ancient Egyptians?" he wanted to know once she was beside him and staring at some faint colored marks on the wall.

"Not really." Jennifer decided to be honest. "And I don't want to learn now. Let's go back to the surface—this place gives me the creeps."

She turned, waiting for him to direct the

flashlight beam back toward the passageway. Instead, she felt his hand come down on her shoulder and pull her toward him. "Oh, for heaven's sake, Franz," she snapped, "this is no time to play games."

"I'd be the first to agree with you, Jennifer." His voice was cool. "And I have no intention of such a childish practice. Unfortunately, you've meddled in a business that doesn't concern you, and the people I work for don't like leaving any witnesses around."

He heard her sharp indrawn gasp and paused to let his words sink in. The faint beam of light coming from the flashlight he held waist-high put strange shadows on his face—shadows which matched the menacing quality of his flat voice as he went on. "I told them you were no danger to us, but there is too much money involved in our Malta operation to take the slightest risk of identification. That's why we had to make sure that Elias died." Franz saw her eyes widen in alarm, but he continued querulously before she could interrupt. "All the fool had to do was deliver the explosive to the tower. His first mistake came when he took you along; the second was when he lied about it later."

Franz's voice echoed sonorously around the gloomy chamber as he delivered the indictment. Jennifer stared at him as if hypnotized, unable even to take a faltering step backward. His original announcement startled her beyond belief, but, after that, his words had merely confirmed suspicions she had harbored uneasily from the beginning.

She stared up at his shadowed features. "You were the man in the tower." Her words finally came out in a rush. "It's that robe you have on—I should have noticed before when you were leading me down here. And the way you hurried past the pyramid . . . it was the same bobbing motion when you ran away in Malta."

"There is a stiffness in one leg." He sounded annoyed at having to explain any physical imperfection. "It was the result of a wound from our first operation."

"For the terrorists?"

"The newspapers have applied many names to our group. It really doesn't matter. In the end, we shall succeed."

"Not if everyone makes as many mistakes as you have. If I'd had any sense, I wouldn't have tried to find excuses for you. On the car ferry— you knew about that loose cargo container because that crewman warned you about it. That's why you shoved me out on deck alone, wasn't it? In hopes that I'd blunder into something."

"You showed an aptitude for such things," he said callously. "There was no harm in trying. I even managed to help save you, once Whitney came on the scene. So that only left Egypt. When you obligingly appeared on the steps of the hotel this morning"—he shrugged—"the rest was painfully easy. And now we have talked long enough." His smile was a brief, wolfish gleam. "Enough to satisfy your curiosity. By the time you're discovered down here, I will be on a flight out of the country. Unfortunately, my Foundation job cover has to be abandoned, but I won't be sorry to leave that fool Edwin and his middle-aged courtesan."

Jennifer saw the shine of metal as he reached under his robe to pull a knife from his waistband. She gasped and glanced frantically around, weighing her chances of reaching the tunnel.

Franz didn't attempt to hold her by him; he appeared to welcome some macabre excitement before disposing of her.

Such obvious sadism made outraged defiance flare in the woman beside him. "You're not as smart as you think," Jennifer said, fighting to keep her voice steady as she accused him. "There's going to be an eyewitness no matter what you do here. Elias isn't dead. Reed found that out from his call to Malta this morning. By now, I'll bet they've sworn out a warrant for you. You'll never get out of Egypt."

"You're lying," he spat out.

"No, I'm not." Somehow she found the courage to continue. "You'd be a fool to risk an Egyptian murder charge on top of all the rest. Think of all the witnesses who saw us drive away from the hotel."

When Jennifer saw his thick figure stiffen in reaction, she knew that she'd lost her gamble. Her own body tensed as he started toward her, the knife ready at his side. Instinctively, she pivoted—in a last desperate chance to escape when Reed's strident call came from the tunnel.

"Jennifer! Are you all right! For god's sake—answer me!"

Franz whirled, momentarily turning the light toward the entranceway. In the instant he relaxed his vigilance, Jennifer brought both her forearms down hard on his hand holding the flashlight. Surprise rather than force weakened his grip, and the light plummeted to the stone floor with a loud shattering of glass, its beam gone.

Franz swore violently in German as he blundered in the dark, his frantic muttering leaving no doubt of his intentions once he got his hands on her. Jennifer cowered in a corner of the chamber, terrified that he'd find her before help arrived.

Then, as other masculine voices mingled with Reed's outside, Franz made a frantic dash toward the tunnel, his steps fading away as he started up the incline.

Jennifer let out her breath and stayed where she was. It was impossible to do anything else since her arms and legs were still trembling uncontrollably. Edwin found her there when he descended into the chamber a moment or two later with an oil lantern held above his head as he peered nearsightedly into the gloom.

Jennifer managed to push herself erect and went slowly to meet him. "You look like Diogenes searching for an honest man," she said with an unsteady laugh. "Would I do instead?"

He sensibly ignored that. "Are you all right, my dear?"

"I'm much better now than I was five minutes ago." She tried to peer through the shadows behind him. "I thought I heard Reed . . ."

"Oh, you did." Ed lowered the lantern to his side. "He's helping the Inspector get Franz back to the car. It took both of them to drag him away."

Jennifer was wide-eyed. "But how did you know I was here?"

"Because we saw you leaving the hotel. Reed and I had just breakfasted there with Inspector Nefer—he's in charge of one of our police inspection teams on the Nile. Reed was telling us what he'd learned from the Embassy's call to Valletta. The Maltese authorities are trying to protect their star witness by letting the newspapers leak the story of his 'death.' You see, Elias had identified the leaders in the terrorist ring before that—Franz among them. Incidentally, Franz was the one who made the attempt on his life. The police have also found the bombs." Ed's smile was benevolent. "Not in the oil rig, as you suspected. They'd planted them in another textile factory this time, owned by an

Italian firm. The oil rigs were targeted for their next attempt." He saw her sway slightly as if overcome by the news and said quickly, "I'll take you to the car now—I should have done it right away."

Jennifer didn't underestimate the man. "But you thought it would be less disturbing to wait until Franz was safely out of sight." She smiled slightly. "Thank you. I appreciate it."

"It's the least I can do. I told Reed on the way out here that I should have been suspicious long before this. That day in Valletta at lunch, Franz professed to know all about the attack on you because he'd discussed it with Louise. It wasn't true at all. She hadn't seen him earlier that day. We seldom saw him all the time he was there. Not my idea of a proper assistant at all." Edwin sounded suddenly like his usual persnickety self, but it was so nice and normal that Jennifer could have hugged him.

There was another interruption at that point which changed her way of thinking. Reed burst into the chamber, his chest heaving from his run down the long tunnel. He pulled up abruptly at seeing Jennifer standing there, and the look of utter relief that passed over his drawn face made Edwin turn and disappear up the incline, tactfully leaving his lantern behind.

Then Reed took three more strides and yanked Jennifer into his arms. She could feel his reaction as their bodies came together and she unashamedly burrowed even closer, reveling in his male strength.

Reed's hands went over her roughly and urgently, as if he needed convincing that she was really there—where she was meant to be. "Dear god," he muttered unsteadily, "I lived through a million years trying to get here. If that damned little vulture touched a hair of your head . . ."

"Darling—he didn't." There would be plenty of time later to tell him what had happened. All she wanted then was to stay in that passionate embrace, pulsingly aware of the heat of his body through his thin shirt as she clung to him. "Don't ever go away again," she managed to say while she still had a chance.

"I haven't the slightest intention of going away," he murmured next to her ear. "You should have figured that out when I dug up all those feeble excuses in Madeira about needing a secretary. I thought we'd get to know each other properly on this trip. Instead"—she could see the taut way he was holding his jaw to keep his voice steady—"I almost got you killed." There was such undisguised anguish in his expression that her heart pounded and her hands went up to pull his mouth within reach.

"Don't think about it," she whispered. "I'm not going to. There are so many nice things to remember. Why do you imagine I listened to all of those feeble excuses for a secretary in the first place? Even Jeremy suspected, because I'm a terrible typist."

"You can use one finger so far as I'm concerned," Reed whispered against her lips. "Provided you start practicing on a marriage license this afternoon."

It was three days later before they were able to fly back to the island of Madeira where it had all started. By that time, they had managed to find an understanding Anglican clergyman in Cairo who had smoothed all the formalities. When they drove up to Reid's Hotel in Funchal on an early Thursday evening, Jennifer had been Mrs. Reed Whitney for approximately twelve and a half hours. "This is where I came in," she protested to the tall man beside her. "I think you must own stock in an airplane company. You're sure we can spend a whole week here this time?"

"Certainly we can. I happen to have a very sentimental attachment to this hotel."

"You looked very much attached to that blonde stewardess in the lobby when I met you here the last time."

"So you remembered." Reed grinned complacently. "A very nice girl. Too bad her last husband misunderstood her." He waited until their cab stopped and then opened the door and helped Jennifer out. "If you like, I'll tell you the story of her life later tonight."

"You don't mind if we have a swim first?" Jennifer's tone was deceptively mild.

"Not in the least. Or we can drive up to that nightclub we visited the last time you were here."

"I'd suggest you go and register before we need two rooms."

He didn't bother to reply to that, merely giving her a grin that made her drop her glance in confusion.

She was still trying to recapture her dignity when he advised that she go on up to their room along with the luggage. "I'll be with you in a few minutes," he said. "There are a couple things I have to do."

Jennifer nodded obediently and headed for the elevator. When she was installed in their room, and she'd heaved a happy sigh over a vase of fragrant coral roses which Reed had ordered, she found herself wondering what was keeping him in the lobby. Then she shrugged and opened her suitcase to start unpacking.

She heard her husband's knock on the door a few minutes later and went to admit him.

He came in clutching a four-foot fur camel nonchalantly under his arm. The scruffy but endearing beast wore a frayed pink ribbon around his neck with an official fumigation notice dangling from it. "I had to collect your wedding present," Reed said. "Edwin and Louise shipped him from Alexandria."

"I knew I'd been missing something all along," said Jennifer, going over to inspect her present. "What a lovely surprise!"

Reed was picking stray pieces of fur from his sleeve. "It must be the moulting season for camels." He dropped the last bit in the waste basket and reached out to pull his bride into his arms. "Come here, madam—you can admire him later."

Jennifer cooperated enthusiastically, slipping her arms under his sport coat and standing on tiptoe to plant a kiss on his chin. "Mmmmm! You're wonderful!" she murmured. "I don't blame that blonde for falling for you."

"There was a gorgeous brunette waiting for the elevator, but she left when I approached with our dromedary friend. I can see what'll happen to my social life from here on." He waited for Jennifer's quiver of laughter to subside before he asked, "Have you decided what you want to do for the rest of the night?" The last words were muffled because he was busy kissing the soft hollow in her throat.

Jennifer found it took remarkable presence of mind even to answer, as his lips worked farther down the V-neckline of her blouse. "What's our choice?"

"Well, there's a program of native dances on the terrace," he said, disposing of a button that was hampering his progress, "or a discotheque on the roof." His hand moved expertly and he felt her tremble in response, but he kept his voice solemn. "Of course, we could just have a swim and then go to bed . . . whatever you say." After that, he began to kiss her in earnest.

It was considerably later before they reluctantly drew apart. By unspoken but unanimous consent, the swim had been abandoned.

There was another brief delay while Reed tucked the camel in the closet and closed the door. "Very tactful beasts—camels," he reported, returning to the bedroom where his bride was waiting. "Now where was I?"

"Just come over here," she invited softly, "and I'll let you know."

About the Author

Glenna Finley is a native of Washington State. She earned her degree from Stanford University in Russian Studies and in Speech and Dramatic Arts, with emphasis on radio.

After a stint in radio and publicity work in Seattle, she went to New York City to work for NBC as a producer in its international division. In addition, she worked with the "March of Time" and *Life* magazine.

As a producer, she had her own show about activities in Manhattan, a show that was broadcast to England. The programs were similar to those of the "Voice of America."

Though her life in New York was exciting, she eventually returned to the Northwest where she married. Currently residing in Seattle with her husband, Donald Witte, and their son, she loves to travel, and draws heavily on her travels and experiences for the novels that have been published. Her books for NAL have sold several million copies.